VIKING FIRE

Andrea R. Cooper
author of *The Garnet Dagger*

CRIMSON
ROMANCE
F+W Media, Inc.

This edition published by
Crimson Romance
an imprint of F+W Media, Inc.
10151 Carver Road, Suite 200
Blue Ash, Ohio 45242
www.crimsonromance.com

Copyright © 2013 by Andrea R. Cooper

This is a work of fiction. Names, characters, corporations, institutions, organizations, events, or locales in this novel are either the product of the author's imagination or, if real, used fictitiously. The resemblance of any character to actual persons (living or dead) is entirely coincidental.

ISBN 10: 1-4405-7122-8
ISBN 13: 978-1-4405-7122-0
eISBN 10: 1-4405-7123-6
eISBN 13: 978-1-4405-7123-7

Cover art © 123rf.com

To my Grandmother (McLaughlin) Hyde, who was proud of her heritage, and instilled that same curiosity in me. She never knew that Vikings might have been part of our ancestry, but she would have loved that. Her childhood stories of her feisty temperament were my inspiration for the heroine and this story.

To my husband who not only showed me love is real, but opened up a world of magic and fantasy. Who encouraged me to indulge in my love of reading, and never told me to give up my dream of becoming a writer. And who wrestled with little ones so I had time to write. Thank you for your support. I love you.

To my children, Troy, Levi, and Chloe, may you always follow your dreams, and hold onto them until they come true. Never accept defeat even when friends or family doubt you.

Acknowledgments

A special thank you goes to Jennifer Lawler for giving me and this story a chance. Thank you to Ashley Myers who bled my manuscript like a ravenous vampire, but through her guidance it was reborn into a better version. The Crimson Romance editors, for polishing my story further and inspiring me to make my writing better. Thank you Crimson Romance staff for helping my story reach others.

Thank you to my writing group, friends, family, and strangers who supported me by listening to my ramblings about this book, or reading it and offering insights.

Enormous gratitude to my sister, Pam, who helped me take this story further.

Chapter One

Ireland 856 CE

"I renounce Father for this." Kaireen threw the elderberry gown. Dressed only in her leine, she glared at the new gown on the stone floor.

"Shame on you and your children for speaking such." Her handmaid, Elva, gathered the damask and then dusted off the rushes. "It's a wonder one of the clim has not scolded you from your hearth for such talk." She wore her white hair twisted in a chignon, underneath a linen head cloth. Strands of white hair poked out the sides of her covering.

"No, curse Father for a fool." She plopped on her bed and a goose feather floated away. With a huff, she leaned against the oak headboard. Red curtains puffed like a robin's chest around oak poles supporting her wooden canopy.

Her bare feet brushed against the stone floor. Why was she not born plain like her two older sisters? Already they had married and expected their second bairns by spring. Well, at least so far she had enjoyed twenty years of freedom.

Three years longer than her sisters. Her parents had her sisters married by their seventeenth birthday. Marriage at such a late age was uncommon, but her father had wanted suitable matches. They had enjoyed freedom longer than others. Many women were given in marriage soon after their first woman's cycle.

Neither of her sisters had had matrimonial dreams of love matches. Both were arranged marriages. Margaret was married to an O'Neill. They courted through the long winter and past the blooming of spring with an early summer wedding.

Two months later he roamed other women's skirts, finding too many others who were willing. Margaret's irritation was lessened as she was ensured by the Laird O'Neill's formal letter that no bastard would have claim to her husband's land or rights if she were widowed.

Her other sister, Shay, and her husband did not set eyes upon each other until the wedding feast. Then they were never separated until tragedy ripped them apart.

Four months ago, her husband was killed in an unexpected skirmish against another clan. Shay refused to admit his death—until his blood-soaked body arrived with his clansmen.

For days she refused to eat or drink. Her salvation was she carried their second unborn child in her womb, and their two-year-old daughter needed a mother. The wee bairn was due this month. Kaireen feared that without the children, her sister would have wasted away without her love.

Often she wondered what her life would be like with a love like Shay's. A love so strong it threatened her sister's life . . . or would she prefer Margaret's marriage, without love and faithfulness?

"You know your da arranged a marriage within a season." Elva smirked.

Kaireen shook her head. "To another land holder," and waved a hand in disgust, "not t-this heathen. Twice they raided our land in the last month alone." She slapped away a strand of her auburn hair from her face. "Their forces choke the land like the town of Ath Cliath, the hurdled ford they call Dubhlinn." This was in reference to the bank of wooden hurdles the Vikings built across the Liffey River. Recent whispers of a possible spy in their midst sent shivers down Kaireen's back. What if this foreigner was the spy? What if he had fooled everyone in her clan?

Well, she would not have the wool pulled over her head by likes of a Lochlann.

"Many a raid has come from them. Now father wants me as wife to one of them?" She clenched her fists. "No, I will not marry this Viking or as we call his kind from west Scandia-Lochlanns." She snatched the green hazel twig from Elva's outstretched hand. Then she scrubbed her teeth.

When the foreigners had first attacked Ireland, they had been called Gaill. Over time the distinction grew between Gaills, Lochlanns, and Normanni depending on what part of Scandia they swooped down from.

Elva smiled, reminding Kaireen of the rumors of her handmaid's uncanny foresight. Whispers of Elva making strange things happen and often blamed as the cause of Kaireen's stubborn refusal to behave as a laird's daughter should.

Kaireen tossed the twig in the fire burning in the hearth. After taking the woolen cloth Elva handed her, she wiped her teeth.

"You've not seen him yet." Elva wiggled her brows.

"So?" Kaireen shrugged. "I would like to never see him." She scrubbed her teeth again with the woolen fabric, and then set the cloth aside.

"Well then, would you not like to know if you have a handsome husband or not?" She waited for her response, but Kaireen scowled at her. Elva chuckled. "I would rather get a good look at him now than the morning after."

Kaireen's ears heated. "I am not marrying." She shook her head for emphasis. "So there will be no morning, nor night, nor wedding."

"If he is handsome, I may fight you for him." Elva smiled, deepening the wrinkles around her eyes.

"Welcome to him either way." Kaireen laughed.

"Careful." Elva winked. "Love makes us fall hardest when we have no intention of doing so. "Especially if stubbornness or pride is involved." She fluffed the damask gown. "Up with you now. We cannot have you going for supper in your leine."

"With or without my leine, I do not go willingly." Kaireen rose. She allowed Elva to yank the violet gown over her head. She pushed her arms through and her clenched hands emerged out of the long sleeves.

She brushed her pale hands down the front of the pile-weaved material. She squared her shoulders and then slipped on her leather shoes.

Plopping on her wooden stool, she suffered though Elva fixing her hair.

As Elva brushed her auburn mane, she fidgeted. Despite refusing to marry this foreigner, her stomach did a flip at the thought. *After all the Lochlanns are good for nothing but raping and pillaging!* To be safe, she would bring her dagger with her. It was waiting for her on top of her cherry wood chest. She tucked the nervousness away as her being hungry. Her handmaid twisted her locks and weaved ribbons within the waist length strands.

Then she secured the end with a ribbon sewn with pearls. Elva gestured for her to rise. Kaireen did so reluctantly.

"Stand straight," Elva snapped.

Kaireen frowned but obeyed. At least Elva was better than her mother's handmaid, Rhiannon. Ever since Rhiannon came to the keep fifteen years ago, she had given Kaireen nightmares. Kaireen would have asked the fairies to put a changeling in her place if she had to have her care. Her mother tried to explain why they had accepted her into their clan being that she was an O'Neill, but Kaireen had tuned her out. She did not care where the woman was from or why.

"And stop scowling or I will throw you out the window with the chamber pot waste."

Her stomach tightened, but she bid Elva goodnight. She hiked up her gown to avoid tripping and then marched the corridor to the great hall.

Through her slippers, she felt the cold of the stone floor. A draft of wind coursed through her and she shuddered. She rounded the corner and forced her arms to her sides. She must appear strong and unnerved. Her arguments would hold no bearing if she could not stop shaking from fury.

...

Inside the banquet hall, the tables were covered with spiced apples, roasted carrots, asparagus, wild duck, quail, and foul smelling pig. Her father and mother sat next to each other at the middle of the high table.

Various lords, barons and their wives along with sons and daughters, laughed at an amusing story her father told. Three hunting dogs scampered around, devouring falling morsels. In a corner lay a fourth dog, shaggier than the rest gnawing on a bone.

Kaireen strolled to the low table, taking the empty seat on the bench across from her parents. Her favored place on her father's left was already taken by a stranger with golden hair, the Lochlann stared at her. Kaireen felt the urge to check the neckline of her gown, but stifled it. A servant girl refilled his goblet with ale.

Kaireen glanced back at him. Golden hair cascaded to his broad shoulders. His azure eyes unsettled her. Her breath caught in her throat and she jerked her head away from his gaze. Didn't the priest say something like "Breton, the devil that dragon often disguises himself as an angel of light." She had no desire to find out from which side of Sidhe, the fairy haven, this stranger sailed from.

Silently she admonished herself to stop playing the role of a child. Thought Elva might find him handsome, well, most women would. She heard women's gowns rustle as they leaned forward to catch a glimpse of the man from across the seas. The way these women gasped at his sailing story, any moment one of them would faint. Did they forget so soon that he was a Viking? One of many who ravaged their land, sacked their monasteries at best, and took women and children as slaves. Some of the women were fortunate enough not to be raped, others were not so lucky.

Her ears burned when the Lochann's resonant voice told of the fiery red dragon he tamed sailing their coast. Did her father tell him that he had always teased her that it would be easier for him to raise a red dragon then a red-haired daughter?

Her insides twisted as the Lochlann finished spinning his tale. She would not look at him again tonight. What did she care what his appearance was anyway. She took a sip of wine, glancing at the stranger over the rim.

He winked at her and she choked.

As the baroness on her left twisted, the bench creaked. She pounded Kaireen on the back with her palm. Her back bruised from the woman's smacks, she assured the woman she no longer needed assistance.

"What do you think of our country, Bram son of Ragnar?" her mother asked the Lochlann.

"Never seen anything so green. Until I looked into your daughter's eyes which make the trees bow in shame."

"Blasphemous." A blush flooded to the roots of Kaireen's hair.

"No, 'tis truth."

Her father held his cup in a toast. "To Bram, the first man ever to bring a blush to my daughter's cheeks."

Kaireen glowered, her anger filling her.

The hall rang with laughter. She wished for sap to stick their mouths shut.

After the laughter subsided, her father cleared his throat. "Now, now. We must control ourselves. Not every day a man gets his last child married."

"I am not marrying," Kaireen interrupted. "And I am not a child."

"Gracious Bram has agreed to stay on with us for a fortnight. Then he will marry our Kaireen."

The applause was deafening. She jumped off the bench, glaring at the Lochlann's smiling face.

"A fortnight?" she screeched. "Not enough time for me to . . . he is a foreigner and a Lochlann at that." Why did they believe it was suitable for her to marry this Viking? She had to have time to figure out how to get rid of him.

"How much time do you need?" her mother asked in a warning tone.

"Never would be too soon," Kaireen shot back.

"Enough." Her father slammed his fist on the table.

Before the ale spilled, her mother snatched her goblet. Their argument brought whispers through the tables.

Her father waved his drink and the ale sloshed on the linen tablecloth. "A fortnight was his idea. I wanted you wed tonight." Kaireen opened her mouth to protest, but his glare caused her to clamp it shut. "Further, you will wed Bram son of Ragnar and be happy about it. Or I will have you whipped until your ungrateful hide is stripped from you."

Kaireen fell on the bench with a groan. She did not need to look to know the Lochlann was beaming. Curse them all for fools. With her knife she pushed her piece of duck around on the trencher. She would not submit, no matter how much her father yelled.

After they finished the other five courses, her father ordered the musicians brought in. Servants scrambled to remove the tables and benches, making room for the dancers. The high table remained.

At Kaireen's orders, the servants placed her bench near the back of the high table so she faced away from the dancers.

The baroness continued to eat beside her; it was the subject of many jokes she would not finish her supper until the kitchens were empty.

Three lute players, and a harpist played the round dance song.

Soon, Kaireen tapped her foot to the rhythm. She watched her father and mother, along with many of the other guests, whirl through the hall changing partners within the lines. The foreigner danced among them.

The oldest woman grinned, as though he were her suitor when he took her arm. Rebecca, a year younger than Kaireen, circled around twice in a row with him.

"It matters not to me who he dances with. Maybe he will change his mind and marry her," she muttered.

She smirked, envisioning his astonishment at learning that Rebecca's dark mane was a wig. Rebecca's hair, a stringy brown, had been chopped off three years ago. No one knew exactly why, but ever since her bout of sickness, patches of baldness showed through her hair, which refused to grow again.

But Kaireen's eyes followed him across the floor. He released Rebecca into the women's line. After he turned, he waved for Kaireen to join him. She whipped her head back to face the table.

Her skin prickled. She bit her lip, suppressing the notion that she had been caught staring. She snatched a piece of duck and ate.

The baroness stood and Kaireen held onto the bench to keep from falling to the floor. The music changed twice while Kaireen was brooding, but she determined she would not turn around again. She would wait until the next song, and then retire. Therefore, he would know she was neither afraid nor interested in him.

Across the room, she heard Rebecca's laughter. She wanted to scream and rip the girl's wig off, exposing her. However, she remained in her seat, her back rigid.

She congratulated herself on her discipline, when Elva appeared from nowhere at her side.

"Must not let the night pass without a dance." She pulled on Kaireen's elbow.

"I have no wish to," Kaireen protested.

Her voice fell on deaf ears, for Elva yanked her to stand.

Her handmaid pushed her forward. Kaireen's slippers slid across the stone floor as she tried to dig in her heels.

"Stop, or I will have you locked in the stocks." She turned her head to yell at her handmaid.

A male hand grasped her arm and escorted her through the line. Her attention shifted as she glared at a beaming Elva. She saw her handmaid skip from the hall.

Then Kaireen glanced at her partner.

Bram held her.

She tripped, but he steadied her. His hands were warm.

"Careful." His dark sapphire eyes twinkled. She wondered if one could drown gazing up into their depths. "People will think you swoon for me."

Her face heated with anger, she believed her skin colored purple. She stamped her foot on his boot, but he did not flinch. She tried to jerk away from his grip, but he held her firmly.

"Let me go." She looked around for help, but everyone had given them a wide berth. They danced around the pair, smiling and nodding as if she and Bram were a happy couple. "'Tis my turn in the line again."

"No." He led her to the balcony.

Outside he released her, but blocked her path to re-enter the hall.

The music resonated around them. Leaning against the far wall, she crossed her arms. She was two feet away from him, but he was too close.

"I thought the air would clear your head." He cocked his eyebrow, examining her.

"My head is fine, thank you."

"Aye, and the rest of you is fine to look at too." His thick dialect chased shivers through her.

Her hands smoothed her gown. She caught herself and stopped. At seeing his grin, her frown deepened. "I believe it's improper for you to stare at a lady so."

"Would you rather I stare at you on our wedding night?" She opened her mouth to speak, but he continued. "Whilst you are without clothes?"

"I assure you, sir, we will have no wedding night." Her blush radiated from her chest and spread between her legs.

"You wish to wed during the day then?" He took a step closer. "Very well, daylight will be all the better to see you."

Music and laughter from inside filtered through the night air. He strode toward her.

She braced for his advances, wondering if she had the strength to inflict enough pain to make him reconsider. Part of her wanting to run, the other part daring him closer in challenge. God's toenails, how could she have forgotten her dagger?

A breath from her, he stopped. Her heart hammered in her chest.

His fingers brushed aside a strand of her auburn hair that had slipped from her braid.

The brief touch sent fire coursing through her. Afraid her legs would give way she leaned back against the wall. He did have a wonderful smile though, with full lips and small white scar that went from his lower lip to his chin.

If he kissed her, she would like nothing more than to bite through those lips leaving another scar far worse than the one he already bore. Or her dagger would have been enough to keep his lips at bay. Why had she forgotten it when Elva dressed her?

Best to make him leave, and soon. He watched her for what felt like an eternity.

"Sir, you take far too many liberties." Her eyes darted behind him at the dancing. Rebecca craned her neck to see what they did outside the great hall unescorted. "Others . . . " Kaireen began, but she stopped seeing anger flare in his eyes.

"I take none." His mouth firmed. "You are to be my wife. I take liberties with no one else."

His voice stung her. He spun on his heel and left her gaping after him.

Chapter Two

Dawn colored the sky in oranges and pinks as Kaireen strode to the manor's bathing chamber. Her father had invited many to stay the night, and Kaireen wanted to bathe before anyone woke, especially Bram. She smiled. Since she was a child, she was usually the first one awake.

The sun was rising, and there was plenty of time for her to bathe and dress before anyone stirred in their beds.

A fresh green gown and leine draped her left arm, her slippers in her hand. Her other hand carried a beeswax candle mounted on an iron candleholder.

The flame flickered across the corridor, elongating her shadow behind her.

She was grateful to bathe as often as she wished; daily if she desired. Ahead of her, she had sent Elva to prepare the bath. No doubt by now her handmaid had heated the water and filled one of the baths.

Inside the room, she set her candle on a wooden bench. Three huge barrels stood waiting. Six people could fit into each barrel.

As a child, she recollected her family often had guest join them for a public bath. Many families offered this hospitality. Her parent's bathing room was in the middle of the keep, instead of near the kitchens as in other laird's homes.

Kaireen saw steam rolling off the barrel next to her. She set her clean clothes on the bench next to the candle. With her finger, she tested the water. Perfect.

She shrugged from her robe and was about to remove her nightdress, when she heard a male voice behind her.

"The water may have cooled some, but I enjoy a hot bath."

She whipped around.

Bram faced her with a towel tied around his waist, covering the lower half of him. His blond hair was wet and she watched the path of the water trail his muscular chest.

A scream choked her and she snatched her robe to shield her body from his vision.

"I hope to rid you of your shyness on our wedding day." He chuckled. "We will have many baths together after we wed."

"No. Take your leave or I will summon the guards to remove you." She backed away, but her legs knocked against the bench.

Her iron candleholder wobbled. She dashed for the candle, catching the wick and snuffed the flame.

"Allow me." His voice made her stomach flip, or maybe she was becoming ill.

She grabbed her candle holding the wick at arm's length for him to light.

At his stare she tightened her hold on her robe. His hand brushed hers as he touched his flame to her candle.

As soon as her wick caught, she stepped back. The flame wavered, then straightened.

"Are you done? I would like to bathe in solitude and not with a heathen gawking at me."

He stood a breath away from her. His presence sent shivers through her. Must be the earliness of the morning, she thought. Her mind had gone daft.

"Take your bath, my lady." He waved an arm across the filled barrel ignoring her insult. "And at sunrise I will meet you in the courtyard."

She huffed regaining her senses. "I am not some servant for you to order about."

"If I do not have your promise you will meet me,"—his eyes twinkled with mischief—"then I will wait here while you bathe and dress. Then afterward, drag you outside." His eyes challenged her to argue.

She clenched her jaw, refusing to answer.

"I take your silence for your consent." He bowed his head. "I will send Elva as escort when you have finished." He drifted from the room.

Minutes passed as her ears strained for a sound, she checked the hallway, making sure he did not lurk about.

She disrobed and then stepped into the water. The scent of him carried in the bath beneath the lye and wood ash. With the fluid soap she washed as she grumbled that she did not care what he smelled like. She rushed through her bath—she could not relax. Every creak worried her of his return.

She stepped from the barrel and then dried. Instead of waiting for Elva, she threw on her leine and then her gown.

Swiftly Elva swept in, carrying a hazel twig, woolen cloth, and a silver comb in one hand, and a piece of red cloth in the other.

"Morning, my lady." She handed her the stem. Her words sounded as if she sung her mistress a tune.

Kaireen snatched the twig, eyeing the silk as if it might leap from Elva's arm and bite her. Without Elva telling her, she knew the material was a sample for her wedding dress. "Why did you not tell me he was here?"

"He is a handsome man, do you not think?" She laid the crimson material that was only the size of her arm across an empty bench. "The dye-makers did an excellent shade of red from the kermes. I will start work on your wedding gown today. Be finished by your wedding."

"Answer me!"

"He bathed when I arrived to fill your bath." She shrugged. "How was I to know he lingered?"

Kaireen huffed. But she held no doubt Elva told him she came to heat water for her mistress.

Maybe she had woken him so he could harass her.

As she cleaned her teeth with the hazel, Kaireen pondered how to be rid of him.

Then she wiped her teeth with the woolen cloth as Elva pulled the comb through her auburn hair. Her handmaid braided her hair in one long rope and secured the end with ribbons.

Sunlight peered through the arrow slits, filling the room. Kaireen stamped her feet into her slippers. She dipped her fingers into the rose oil and then pressed her damp fingers to the hollow of her throat.

Elva snuffed out the candle with her fingertips. She gathered her mistress's sample for her wedding gown including the silver comb leaving the rest for the scullery maids to clean, and then ushered her outside to the courtyard where Bram waited.

Kaireen followed after Elva. Her mind raced as to how she might escape this. With her temper, the convent would not take her in. Maybe she could wed in secret to someone else beforehand, but she had found fault in her mind of any would be suitor.

Outside, she blinked adjusting to the light. Bram's blond hair glowed in the sunlight. He wore blue hoses and a lighter shade overtunic. His leather belt held a sheathed sword. She flushed remembering the muscles she had seen there earlier.

Her handmaid curtsied to them both. She would serve as chaperone until another took her place.

They walked to the edge of the courtyard where a stone bench sat underneath an oak's spreading limbs. The dark green leaves fluttered in the cool wind. Elva seated herself on the bench and set to work on embroidering the sample material with different designs to find one that Kaireen liked.

His smile warmed her, but she refused to smile back. Perhaps if he was not the believed spy, he was sent by the traitor to investigate their lands. Why else would he demand to see her lands so soon? An attack from there could be devastating as it would not be expected.

He held two pieces of toast. "Break your fast with me?"

"I would rather break fast with a kelpie, and take a drowning ride on its back to the depths of the River Shannon."

"I can dunk you as easily, but you might need something to have the strength to fight me off."

She huffed, but snatched one of the pieces he offered. While she nibbled, she refused to look up at him. They stood in silence eating. The wind shifted through the trees. Leaves rustled, hinting of autumn.

"Your father's guards will escort us through your land." His eyes focused on her face and she wondered why he stared at her so. "He says your dowry's not far from here."

Her land spread to the cliffs and met the pounding waves. Maybe luck would grace her and Bram would fall off the cliff and swim back to his land. "Since my lord father wishes, I will escort you." Kaireen said.

He cocked his head to the side, examining her as if judging her motives.

But she simply smiled at him. The O'Neill clan lived south of her land. They did not take kindly to invaders. She would convince them not to kill him, but only to send him back to where he came from. Of course she would need to find an excuse to be away from her father's guards long enough to get Bram close enough to the border. Perhaps a stroll in the woods? It would be easy to pretend she saw something in the distance, a child? She would come up with something, a distraction to get away long enough for her plan to work.

Kaireen ordered Elva to fetch their cloaks. As they waited they finished their toast. Kaireen stole glimpses of him. Aye, she thought, he was handsome to the eyes. Blond hair with strands of gold and copper filtered through the locks sweeping to his collar. Deep blue eyes contrasted with his skin darkened from the sea and sun.

He caught her stare and she jerked her head away, willing Elva to hurry.

After counting a hundred oak leaves, she saw Elva carrying their cloaks; heavy wool for Bram, and a black pile-weave for Kaireen.

They donned their cloaks. Another servant brought two saddled horses.

...

Across the rolling hills, Kaireen led him on horseback. Five of her father's guards rode with them.

Side by side, she and Bram rode through the land. Bram spoke of his hopes in Ireland; hopes of raising a family, and plenty of land for farming. He would join his forces with her father's as protection against raiders, both Viking and Irish. Squabbles among clansmen were often bloodier than Viking raids. She didn't care that he would help defend against her enemies, not too long ago all would have considered him the adversary.

Unable to stop herself, she laughed as he described his first time riding a horse as a child. His facial antics brought tears to her eyes.

After two hours of riding they reached the border of her land and her father's. Her manor stood on the other side of the rolling hill.

At the top of the hill, a cluster of elm trees rose in tight circle. Bram reined in his horse, glancing between the trees and where the manor stood.

"This mound is taller." He scratched his chin. "Better defense, why not build the keep here?"

"Daoine Sidhe." She dusted off her green gown. Looking at his puzzled expression, she knew he did not understand. "Fairies. Everyone knows." She sighed. "A circle of trees or stones means Daoine Sidhe land."

"What has that to do with anything?"

"Bad luck if you build on fairy land. They bring death." She nodded her head. "Steal children, replace them with changelings."

He stared at her like she was mad.

"Well, superstition, anyway. But no servant would enter a place built on Daoine Sidhe land, much less work there."

He nodded, but she had the impression he thought the air had gone to her head.

Her father's guards followed them as they continued. When she was eight summers, her father had built this manor for her. She was the only one of his daughters that he had given land and housing. The roof finished last year, and furniture added earlier in the spring. Her sister's dowries were gold and jewels instead of land.

They dismounted, and Bram tethered their horses to a flowering bush. "It's such a pleasant day, I thought we'd let the horses enjoy it as well."

The guards waited outside sharing stories.

Inside, rushes swamped the stone floor. A scullery maid visited the manor once a week to clean and change the rushes. The frame shaped from wood and earthware. Steps, hearth, and floor carved from stone. They unfastened their cloaks, laying them across a stool in the kitchen.

She showed him through the kitchen, and behind a thick curtain to the private bath.

The sitting room branched from the hall and stairs rose in the corner.

"The bedchambers are upstairs." She pointed.

"Lead the way, then, my lady." He grinned.

His smile did not falter her resolve to be rid of him, instead she stomped each foot on the stone steps. She showed him the larger one first.

"Our room." She waved her hand as she stood at the threshold.

He moved passed her and into the room. Surveying the goose-feathered mattress he turned back to her. "'Tis the first you admit we marry."

"No. I said no such—"

He crossed the distance to her.

He pulled her in his embrace and she went rigid.

She opened her mouth to scream, but as she drew a breath his lips crushed hers. Tingles of warmth crept from inside her to the tips of her toes. Her mind raced, demanding she be free, while her traitorous body melted in his arms. She wished she had brought her dagger with her.

His kiss became gentle and sparked a craving inside her for more. His mouth opened, offering her to taste secrets within. She slackened against him as his tongue played across her lips, stroking them and numbing her thoughts.

He did not force his way further, but ended the kiss with her lips yearning for his.

Then he stepped back. She gasped, horrified. Her hands were clutching his hair and she jerked them away as if he scalded her.

"Your lips and eyes speak of your love." He beamed at her frown. "Now I am sure of your passion for me."

"No." That was enough! He had overstepped his bounds with his prideful arrogant assumptions. "You are mistaken; I wish to never marry you." She would not fall in love with him. No matter his handsome face. She must not allow herself to acknowledge that she liked it when he kissed her. How she wished to be rid of him and all the turmoil he caused. She would never be free if he became the laird over her.

"Aye, your kiss spoke more that you know." He chuckled and held her hand kissing her palm. "In time the rest of you will agree as well." What could he possibly know of her? How could he not see that she despised his kind and would never trust him as her husband and lover?

"You know not of what you speak." She yanked her hand back.

"I know you long for me," he whispered in her ear. "I like seeing your lips swelled and soft from my kisses."

Auch! She should have bitten those lips. In her fuming to be ordered about during her bath, she had left her dagger again.

He strode away from her as her fingers clenched. Aye, Bram was dangerous. Time she gave him a shove.

Chapter Three

Kaireen gathered her skirts and trudged downstairs.

Through the open door the breeze shifted, bringing the smell of the sea. Noticing Bram's cloak gone, she snatched hers from the stool. She dashed into the open air.

Outside, the waves crashed against the rocks. Bram stood near the cliff's edge.

The sea burst open in waves, spewing white foam. She tasted the salt in the air. She came here often to think. On windy days, the sea crashed so high that the droplets fell like rain.

She fastened her cloak. Lifting the hood, she pushed her hair inside.

A foot from Bram she paused. She wondered what he was thinking. His cloak and blond hair billowed, exposing his square jaw line. Minutes passed, but he did not move.

She walked forward until she stood beside him. His eyes were riveted to the ocean.

The wind strained against her and she fought to stand. She looked across the water, pondering what he stared at. Folding her hands she stifled a yawn.

"We are to have company soon."

"Pardon?" She jumped at the sound of his voice.

Seagulls called.

"A ship heads this way." He nodded his head to the waves. "Be here within two hundred strokes or so."

Again she searched the waves. Then she gasped when she saw a dark shadow the size of a coin moving toward them.

"Friends of yours?" she asked.

"No. I recognize the ship; the owner killed my father without honor and refused to pay the wergild owed as recompense." He turned to her. "And with a wench like you in their sights, they would kill me even if I was their king."

She shivered. More Lochlanns was not what she needed. She could tell not how many came, but given the tension etched on Bram's face she knew their number was too great for him and the five guards who came with them to overcome.

Images flashed across her mind of her struggling against a boatful of men. Laughing, ripping at her clothes.

Bram shook her shoulders, bringing away from her vision. "Take your horse and ride. Warn your father." He rotated her around to face her horse. "Ride hard and do not look back."

Without another word she bolted to her horse. She untied her mare and then mounted.

Dread crept into her throat, but she kneed her horse into a gallop. She would not reach her father's holding in time to save Bram or the others.

The thought of Bram dead should make her nonchalant, but she didn't want to be in any way responsible for it. His death especially upon her land would haunt her forever. She racked her brain. Surely she could do something, anything.

The O'Neill's.

She jerked the reins and spun her mare. A short ride from the southeast of her land was the O'Neill clan, and they always had scouts watching for intruders.

She nudged her horse faster. "You may rest when we arrive at the O'Neill's holding."

Minutes dragged. She wondered if the land stretched ahead of her mocked her urgency. Hopefully she would make it in time to save Bram and the others.

She saw the O'Neill monastery on the cliff's edge. It should be one mile more. Her horse leapt a fallen oak nearly unseating her as it traversed across the grassland.

When her mount reached a cluster of beech and ash trees, two large men jumped out.

Her horse reared. Kaireen tugged on the reins. Her horse settled but kept eyes on the men before them. She patted her mare's neck, reassuring her. The two men held swords before her.

"Shame to you, Uaine and Quinlan." She chided. As wide as they were, she wondered how she did not spot them earlier.

"You trespass on our lands." Uaine lowered his sword from her glare. "Our laird's son demands permission to any who may cross our land."

Quinlan's head bobbed in agreement with his brother. Though he was the younger of the two, he towered over his brother.

"'Tis an urgent matter." She shifted in her saddle. "I must speak with your laird at once."

They stared at their feet.

"W-we have our orders. N-none enter." Uaine stuttered.

"Are you both daft?" Her horse pranced sideways. "I have no time for your trifling rules." She leaned forward and kneed her mare into a gallop.

The horse's hooves knocked Uaine backward. As she raced ahead, she heard their shouts behind her. A weeping willow slashed her face, but she tore through the land.

Arriving at the manor, her mare staggered. Her exhausted horse needed no further encouragement to stop.

Kaireen jumped off and tossed the reins to the stable boy. "Walk her. We traveled too far too fast for her to stop now," She rushed to the stairs. "Gather the other horses, ready all of them." He opened his mouth in surprise. "I am Laird Liannon's daughter. Do it quickly and my lord father and your laird will reward you. Now go."

The young boy scampered away, leading her sweating horse.

Through the gateway she rushed past the three guards taking turns swigging ale from a horn.

She raced the path to the manor. At the door, two guards seized her arms.

"Where you think you are going, my lady?" one said while his eyes roved her form.

"I am Kaireen, daughter of Laird Liannon. I must speak with your laird straightway."

"Straightway, say you?" The guard smirked. "Well, our laird takes no commands from a lady. He will send you to the dungeon 'afore you can think to breathe."

The guard hauled her inside to the waiting hall. His comrade made announcement of an intruder wishing to see the laird.

Moments later, Kaireen heard the buzz of voices fill the rafters. Her ears burned, hearing men's voices refer to her as a mad woman.

"Send her in," said a raspy male voice.

Both guards marched her forward by her arms. They entered a hall. Tapestries covered the walls. One at the back of the room held the O'Neill's coat of arms along the edges and a battle scene with an O'Neill laird raising his sword in victory. A fire crackled in the hearth.

Next to the flames, Laird O'Neill reclined in a carved wooden chair. He was an elderly man with white flowing hair that mingled with his beard.

He wore a purple tunic, and a medallion hung from a chain round his neck. It was silver, carved with symbols, curled around an amber stone the size of her palm. The golden color sparkled in the firelight.

Two clansmen stood on either side behind the laird. The first guard who brought news of her trespass bowed low and then exited to take his post outside.

She swallowed. Laird O'Neill reminded her of the stories of druids who once flooded this land.

"Remove your hand from this lady, Aeneas, and return to your post." His hazel eyes weighed her.

The guard next to her dropped her arm. He, too, bowed and then marched away.

"Now my lady, what brings you here without an invitation?"

"Lochlanns, my lord. They come now in ships northwest of here." The fire popped and she jumped. "Ready your soldiers so we may fight them."

"Our men are on watch and saw no ship." The son on the laird's left spoke. "If they do come, then it 'tis not to our lands. Besides, we do not send our men into battle on the word of a woman." His sneer turned her stomach.

"Kaireen, is it not?" the laird asked.

She nodded.

"My youngest son, Feoras. You know of my eldest son, Bearach." He gestured to the man on his right. "Years ago you played soldiers with his sons, Uaine and Quinlan."

Remembering her encounter with them earlier, she reddened.

His laughter faded and his countenance grew serious. "Now, Feoras has raised an interesting statement . . . we don't send men to battle on the word of a woman. What say you?"

"They come to kill our people, take our women and children as slaves or worse." She dusted her gown frowning at the slashes from the tree limbs. "Destroy our monasteries, homes, pillage our treasures. Kill our people or take away us as slaves."

Feoras opened his mouth as though to protest, but the laird raised his, hand silencing him.

"My lady. Surely you know we must protect our own lands." He smiled at her as if she were a frightened horse. "I cannot risk my men to fight your father's battles. Since my reign, we do not war with your clan. But to avoid our offending other clansmen nor will we ally with your father." He shook his head. "No, we will not fight."

Because she came first to the O'Neill clan, her father would be taken unawares if they did not stop the invasion now. She needed the O'Neill's help. Without them to fight, Bram and the guards were dead.

"My laird, these men do not come in peace. My father and family will be killed." She clung to desperation. "My eldest sister is married to your third cousin. Does it not make us family?"

"Aye. But her allegiance is with our clansmen now, not yours. Because of that and your father, these two are the only things allowing me to keep Feoras from locking you in the dungeon." He waved his wrinkled hand as if shooing a fly. "Our men will remain here."

Her head screamed in pain. She wasted time coming all this way. Curse Bram for a fool, he should have fled with her. The laird called for the guards.

She heard their leather boots clomp toward her. They snatched her.

All was lost.

She would never hear Bram's voice again. Screams of the dying echoed in her mind. A miracle if anyone survived.

Miracle? She strained against the guards' hold.

"My lord, another question." The guards jerked her backwards, but her eyes remained on the laird.

He nodded and the guards let go.

"Perhaps I was mistaken of the Lochlanns' intent."

"How so?" He frowned.

His sons stepped forward each grasping their sword hilts.

"Well, our monastery is hidden from the coast. 'Tis miles to the south of our lands."

"So?" Feoras yawned. "They would take the river, or ride across your land. Once again, this does not concern us." He flexed his hands as though wanting to squeeze them around her neck.

She straightened. She would not be bullied into a subservient attitude, not with lives at stake.

"Oh, but their ship sailing along the coast does." Her heart drummed in her ears. This was the last chance. If she could not convince them to fight, then many lives would be lost especially if she was wrong and the Norsemen attacked her family while they were unaware of the danger.

"Your babbling solves nothing. Our monastery is blocked from the sea by steep cliffs," Feoras roared.

The laird held up a hand and his son snapped his mouth shut. But his dark glare bore into her.

"Your monastery's on the coast. Sailors see it from miles away." The flames shifted the shadows along the walls. "Do you think them foolish to sail to my lands, then journey hours to our monastery, when they need only to cross my woods to reach yours? They could raze it like they did the monastery of Iona and others." She smiled at their gasps. "Perhaps I was mistaken earlier. My lands are not in danger, but yours certainly appear to be." Often monasteries were unprotected. Some might post a few guards, but they were outnumbered when the Norsemen came. No one knew when or where they would strike. Gold, precious jewels, religious treasures with little to no defense drew them like bears to honey.

At the laird's nod, Bearach, the eldest son shouted orders to ready their soldiers.

"Well done, my lady." The laird winked at her, as if ignoring Feoras' dispute. "You raised an argument Feoras could not refute."

"My lord, may I ask two more things of you today?"

He answered her with a raised eyebrow.

Men clamored through the halls, Feoras and Bearach joining them.

"Continue." The laird gestured.

"My lord, please give me a weapon and a horse."

The laird gave his sword to Kaireen. "Take the lead with Bearach, but draw back when you meet the enemy," he told her.

After a bow she followed after the men. Her heart raced.

Outside they mounted. Bearach barked orders and then led the galloping horses through the countryside. He pointed to the shortest trail back to her land, back to Bram. Though he was not her desire for a husband, he had done nothing that was deserving of being murdered. Her luck, he would become a ghost to haunt her.

Kaireen raced a borrowed horse to stay with Bearach.

And prayed she was not too late.

Chapter Four

Tree limbs slashed at Kaireen, but she did not care. She urged the horse forward.

O'Neill's raced after her, their horses' hoofs pounded in the distance. The smell of the ocean lingered in the air.

Did she hear shouts echo on the wind? She shivered. Or was the sound the keening of her family's banshee?

To fight back the dread swelling in her chest, she glanced behind her for reassurance. Bearach and the others galloped after her.

Around this group of trees, and she would reach the clearing. After passing the last cluster of fir trees to the clearing, she turned the horse sharp. In the distance she saw Lochlanns battle. She sucked in a breath.

Two of her father's guards lay dead. She scanned the men fighting to find Bram.

The edges of his grey wool cloak lifted with the sea breeze. His body slumped, but his sword wavered to block an attacker's blow.

Kaireen drew the laird's sword. From the weight of the blade, she lost her balance and countered by leaning backward. Sweat trickled down her back.

As her hand clenched the hilt, she nudged her mount forward. She wished she had asked for a bow. How would she lift the sword to do any damage? She raised the sword until her arm shook, but it was only halfway.

Mounted, she slashed the blade at Bram's enemy.

Her teeth rattled from the impact. Blood spurted from the Lochlann's leather helmet. The man sagged forward, knocking Bram down.

Anxious, she twisted her horse round, but jerked the reins to keep the animal steady.

Bram pushed the dead man away. He staggered and kneeled. His left hand clasped his bleeding side. Disoriented from loss of blood, he told her he was not sure if she had aimed her sword at his enemy or at him.

The O'Neill clan rushed in the fight. Metal swords clanked against each other as they fought the Lochlanns. Bearach raised his sword and ran toward Bram.

"No!" Kaireen kicked her horse forward, blocking Bearach. "He fights for us."

Bearach gaped at her, but then nodded. He turned his attention to two giant men treading forward. He muttered under his breath, "Curse this woman for bringing us into a battle between Lochlanns."

It would have been so easy for her to let Bearach rid her of Bram. Just one word and she would be rid of this Lochlann suitor and his quest to marry her. But she couldn't allow it. True, she did not love him-only she could not tolerate the thought of him dead when she could stop it. It would never do to have innocent blood spilled on her account or here.

Blood colored the ground. The copper stench crept into her throat. Another enemy rushed forward with an axe in hand, roaring a battle cry.

The man inches from her when Bram stretched out his sword and pierced the man's gut. Bram then yanked his sword out, his breathing hard. He fell back on the ground at the same time the enemy crumpled.

O'Neills swept the land; they matched the Lochlanns stroke for stroke. But the Lochlanns drew up their shields into a wall.

One slipped away from the attack and headed towards her and Bram.

After dismounting, she heaved the sword with both hands, and wished she had asked for a bow.

Unable to lift the sword higher than her waist, she lunged forward at a warrior from behind. Surprised by her low lunge, the blade caught the warrior in the back of his upper thigh. The thwack of the metal against the bone radiated through her.

The sword went with him as he fell. He was not dead, just injured. He twisted his upper body around to dislodge the sword in his leg.

She bit her lip; now she was weaponless. Doubtful she'd have such luck again using the heavy sword.

"Damn woman!" Feoras raced passed her. With a swift flick, he decapitated the man at her feet.

She bristled and snatched her horse's reins. Surveying the battlefield, she eyed a longbow. After maneuvering with her horse to the edge of the battle, she made her way to the weapon.

After dismounting, she picked up the discarded longbow and a handful of arrows from the dying Lochlann. She tested the weight of the draw, stronger than she liked, but she was grateful of her years of practice with her own bow. She nocked an arrow.

Her nerves made her hands sweat; she fumbled with the arrow several times until the tip slid into place. She took a breath to calm her nerves. If she could not keep her hands steady, her expert marksmanship would do no good. To concentrate, she pushed aside the thought of Bram dead because of her, and then took aim.

Five warriors surrounded Bram and Bearach.

Her arms shook from the force of strength required to draw the bowstring back. Kaireen released the arrow and the tip struck an enemy's neck.

When she saw the arrow hit, she grasped another and sent it sailing. The arrow whizzed through the air and struck another enemy in the arm.

She readied another, but Bearach and Bram had cut down the other men around them.

After Kaireen scanned the area, she sent her last arrow into another enemy's stomach. She cursed.

"Good shots, why are you upset?" Bearach speaking beside her made her jump.

"My aim was off."

"But your arrows hit their mark."

"No." She eyed the bow thinking it refused to cooperate. "I aimed at their hearts."

"Good thing you missed them not entirely and hit us." He chuckled.

"The draw on the bow was stronger than mine." Her muscles pulsed in pain.

Feoras strode to them. He snatched the long bow from her hand and then broke it across his leg. "You damn near got us killed," he spat.

"No." She crossed her arms. "Without my help, you may have lost this battle. I saved you."

"A woman like you should be turned upon her stomach," he smirked, "and given a good lashing by her husband."

"I have no husband." She smiled. "And I do not take orders from loathsome men such as you."

He raised his hand to strike her, but Bearach caught his wrist.

"Do not let her anger you so." Bearach nodded to the shore. "We drove the foreigners from our shore. Look, they scamper like frightened children back to their boat."

Feoras jerked his hand away. He turned on his heel and chased after the departing Lochlanns.

He yelled for the O'Neills to join him and his scattered followers chased after them.

"Halt! Only a coward fights a man when his runs!" Bearach called, but Feoras and the others continued as if they had not heard.

Feoras descended, using the natural breaks in the cliffs to the shore. His sword rose. At the shore, he and the others slashed the fleeing Lochlanns.

He jumped into the Lochlanns' boat and sliced at men holding their hands in surrender. Kaireen turned her head; it was shameful, what Feoras and the others did.

The waves lapped at the dead's blood.

Bearach raced to stop his brother's madness, but the last dying Lochlann capsized the dragon ship. Against the waves, Feoras and the others were left to struggle for air.

Once he reached the water, Bearach waded in. Kaireen bit her lip. If he stepped too deep, then he may lose his footing and drown if he wasn't a strong enough swimmer against the undertow.

Red waves fanned around the boat. Bearach stretched out his arms, hauling Feoras and three others back to the side of the cliff.

Seeing the struggling Lochlann, Bearach waded deeper into the ocean. Bearach went under a few times, but he could not reach the distant Lochlann.

He fought the waves on his way back to the beach. Two of his fellow O'Neills had drowned.

On the wet sand, Bearach drew ragged breaths with the others he rescued. Feoras lay, sprawled out, but breathed.

"Do idiocy like that again," Bearach stood and then shook water like a wolfhound. "And I will leave you to your grave." Bearach returned to the others.

Then he helped Bram to his feet. Kaireen's hands searched for the damage on Bram's chest. His tunic was soaked with blood. She could not tell how much blood was his or the enemy's.

Bram pushed her hands away. The corners of his mouth turned into a frown, but his blue eyes twinkled. "I told you to go to your father." He continued to lean on Bearach for support.

"You are not my lord husband." Her face heated and she strained to hide her smile. "Nor would I obey such a foolish command even if you were."

"We will discuss your disobedience later." Bram shifted his weight and grimaced.

"If not for me, you would be dead." She huffed crossing her arms. "Why are men so thick skulled?"

"No, women are . . . " Bram started to argue. His eyes rolled in the back of his head and he collapsed.

Bearach ordered a travois made. The men scrambled into the forest to obey.

When the men returned, they dragged tree limbs with them. Bearach worked with the others, cutting pieces of the dead Lochlanns' tunics to tie the limbs together. He gave his cloak to spread across the limbs for Bram.

After the cloak secured the travois, Bearach heaved her father's guards' dead bodies onto their horses. Kaireen tied the horses' reins in a line ending with her horse as the lead.

"Ride slow with him." Bearach carried Bram to Kaireen's horse and placed him on the travois.

She nodded and then mounted her horse.

"A little rest and sewing is all he needs." Bearach turned back to the other travois they had crafted to carry their injured. The dead were draped on their horses; it would be a slow journey back for the O'Neills.

Chapter Five

Dusk colored the sky in purples and reds when Kaireen returned to her father's keep. With another glance back at Bram, she sighed.

He had not stirred since he collapsed earlier. It worried her more than facing her father.

Smoke from the chimney drew ringlets against sky.

Kaireen smelled the roasting pig. Her empty stomach rumbled. With a tug of the reins, the horse sauntered to a stop. She dismounted and then checked on Bram. His blond hair was matted to his head with sweat.

To her touch, his skin burned her fingers. Her father's guards gathered around her. "Take him to his quarters."

Two guards bent to obey her command. Another guard untied the travois, and then led her horse to the stable. Kaireen gathered her skirts and chased after the guards carrying Bram.

Past the bailey she spotted Elva. "Come with me." She dragged Elva with her. "Hurry, he is hurt badly." She thought she heard her handmaid chuckle, but the footfalls down the corridor muffled the sound. Noises from the banquet hall filtered through the walls.

They reached Bram's room and the guards eased Bram onto the bed.

His chest rose and fell with shallow breaths. Kaireen thankful for the movement, though his face was pale and dark circles lined his eyes.

Elva shooed the guards and they halted outside the doorway.

"Close the door behind them," Elva directed her.

She raised an eyebrow at the audacity of her handmaid ordering her, but she complied. The wooden door clicked closed.

"Let them guard the door if they must." Elva untied a leather purse from underneath her outer tunic.

Kaireen rushed forward and stood next to the bed. The dark room smelled of burnt hazel and honeyed mead.

"Light all the candles you can find," Elva ordered her.

Kaireen's heart raced with panic. Bram's condition must be serious for her handmaid to instruct her as if she were a commoner.

Kaireen used the flint stone and lit five candles. She gasped when she saw Elva with her dagger in her hand. Why did she have Kaireen's dagger with her?

Her handmaid cut away his blood-crusted tunic. "Bring the candles closer so I can see the damage."

Kaireen rushed to do so. Her face flushed at seeing his naked chest. No, she was not in love with him. Lust, though was another matter entirely. She would never give in to lust or allow herself to be ruled by it, ever.

After dragging a wooden stool next to the bed, she set the candle down. She gathered the other candles and then placed them on the stool as well.

On his side were two jagged gashes.

"Will he d—" She choked. If he died, she knew her father would blame her.

Elva glanced at her. An eternity past until her servant spoke. "No, he will live." She smiled at her mistress's relief. "I have not forgotten the old ways." Elva opened the leather purse, revealing pockets of separated dried herbs. "Bring me the water basin."

Without thought Kaireen obeyed. Elva pinched fragments of brown and yellow herbs into the basin. She swirled the herbs around and whispered words Kaireen did not understand.

A fragrant mixture of hyssop, myrrh, and pine emerged. Still she added more.

Then she lifted her underskirt, revealing a secret holding bag, and removed three vials the size of her palm.

She poured the first two into the bowl, then stirred the ingredients, complaining about consistency.

The third vial she opened with caution. An acrid stench arose.

"Take your dagger and cut strips from his bed linens not covered in blood."

Her dagger fell on the bed next to Bram's right leg.

Kaireen grasped the blade. She wrinkled her nose. But she could not find a spot next to him without blood. She swept to the other side of the bed.

Holding the dagger she cut four strips from the bed linens. Her hands shook. Finished, she brought the strips to Elva.

"Careful." Elva handed her the third vial.

And Kaireen jumped at her handmaid's snap. But she steadied the vial in one hand and the strips and dagger in the other. Holding the vial this close made her eyes water from the pungent smell.

"Douse the wound with this liquid on the cloth. Clean the wound until no blood comes." Elva threaded a needle. "On with it, child."

Kaireen squatted beside Bram. After this Elva would require a thrashing for her behavior. As though unconcerned, Elva threaded a needle.

She poured the liquid onto one of the strips and then wiped his wound. The first two strips were quickly soaked with blood.

If Elva did not heal him, she would have her head. She let her shoulders relax, relieved that blood did not cover the fourth cloth. She sheathed her dagger attaching it to her belt.

"'Tis clean." She turned back to Elva.

Elva nodded, bringing the threaded needle.

"What do you need it for? His wound does not bleed anymore."

"Any movement and his wound will reopen. The liquid is for cleaning, to stop the fever and infection. Also it works well to staunch the bleeding."

Kaireen watched as Elva sewed Bram's wound closed. She cringed each time the needle passed through his flesh. She wondered if it would leave a scar like the others that randomly lined his chest and shoulders in fading lines.

Elva finished. She tied a knot to secure her mending, then bit the extra thread with her teeth.

Elva tested the solution she had made in the water basin. Then she smeared the foul smelling remedy across his stitched wound.

"Cut long strips from his bed linens. Long enough to wrap around his chest."

Kaireen followed her instructions.

Then Elva emptied the water basin into the chamber pot. Yellowish-brown paste covered Bram's wound. Then her handmaid used a little of the salve on Kaireen's cheek where the willow tree had slashed her. The cut burned and she reached her hand up to scratch it when Elva slapped her hand away.

"Leave it be. Call the two guards in," Elva ordered her as she cleaned her hands using the water from a pitcher.

Kaireen almost curtsied, but caught herself and frowned. She stalked to the door and then flung it open. "Come inside," she barked.

They stumbled in.

On her grey livery, Elva dried her hands, the vials of liquids and pouches of herbs hidden. "Lift him so I can bind his wound."

They gaped at Kaireen and she nodded.

Elva wrapped the cloths around Bram and then fastened them closed with a knot.

Kaireen thanked the guards and they left. She waited for hours and no change in Bram's fever or consciousness. Elva disappeared leaving her alone with him. On her handmaid's orders, she smoothed droplets of water on his lips every so often. He did not gain consciousness, but would swallow when she drizzled the water into his mouth.

"Drink." Elva returned and handed her a goblet filled with honey-mead. "You need to rest. It would not do to lose either of you to battle nor blight."

Kaireen wondered where Elva had gotten mead; it was probably Bram's. But her throat was parched and her stomach rumbled. She was in need of peaceful rest, not wanting the demons of the battle to trouble her dreams.

She downed the liquor, but a bitter taste lingered on her tongue as she set the goblet back in Elva's outstretched hand.

Bram moaned.

Concerned, her fingers touched his cheek. Relief—his skin was clammy, but not burning as before. She brushed back his golden hair and flushed, recalling his kiss. The kiss she wanted to slash him for.

But she must not fall in love with this man. He was a Lochlann.

She paced around the room while Elva tidied it up. Once he was healed, she would insist he leave and never return. Her handmaid drew the shutters closed and latched them in place.

Flickering candles provided light in the darkened chambers. Kaireen stared at the flames. They danced with orange and yellow costumes. Dizzy, she swayed on her feet as Elva tossed blankets over Bram.

Then her handmaid stood at her arm pulling her toward the door. "Away with you now." She said. "He needs rest. And you need to eat." Kaireen opened her mouth to protest, but her handmaid interrupted. "I will get soup in him, do not worry. Go to the kitchens and eat the leftover lamb. Cook has some heated. Then you will go straight to bed yourself. You can deal with your parents and husband on the morrow."

Kaireen shook her head, the room spinning. "He is not my husband." Her voice sounded soft to her ears.

"Of course, dear." Elva pushed her out.

Kaireen shuffled into the kitchens, but could not recall her steps there. The cook, a wide woman with spindle legs, carved slices of a leg of lamb, explained Kaireen's good timing as she now had time to re-heat tonight's meal for her supper.

After swallowing a few bites of lamb and stewed carrots, Kaireen staggered to her room.

She kicked the door closed behind her, stumbled and fell across her bed. She strained to keep her eyes open, but sleep won. "I will not fall in love with him." Surely he will be glad to be on his way when he recovers for he must value his life more than a hard-hearted woman.

Chapter Six

Kaireen woke with her auburn hair tickling her nose. Sunlight filtered through the half closed shutters. She groaned. Running a hand through her hair, her fingers caught on tangles. She was dressed in her green tunic with tattered gashes from her ride last night.

Her tongue tasted bitter as she clambered out from bed. Where was Elva?

She glared at the closed shutters. Yanking one side open she squinted from the sunlight, shading her eyes with a hand and gaped. The sun burned high in the sky. It must be past noon.

She snatched a clean shift and gown. She left her room, and stamped down the hallway to the bathing chamber. As she grumbled, her green riding skirts flared around her legs.

On the way she spotted a servant girl. "Ready a bath for me."

The girl curtsied.

"Make the water warm enough. I do not want gooseflesh."

The girl giggled, staring at Kaireen's disheveled hair.

Inside, Kaireen set her clothing on the bench. Muttering she must look a mess, she grabbed a silver comb left for guests and raked it through her hair.

"With your hair tangled, you look a worse sight then me." A male voice sounded to her right.

She whirled around recognizing Bram's voice.

Leaning on a wooden staff, he grinned. His side was bound with fresh linens round his chest. Ends of his golden hair lay damp and brushed against his collarbone. He shifted and then grimaced, as if standing was painful.

She forced her body to stay still. She would not rush into his arms like some milksop girl wanting to kiss his face for living. Instead, she tugged the comb through her tangled mane.

"Careful." He winked. "Else you will have no hair left on your beautiful head."

She winced, jerking out a handful of hair. Did he know about Rebecca, then? She frowned at his smile.

Against the wall he slouched, watching her.

"Are you going to stand there all day?" she asked.

"Until I have strength to make the journey back to my room."

Was he so weak he had to rest?

Where was Elva? Oh, she would skin the woman alive if he fell to sickness from strain after all she went through to save his Lochlann hide.

"Perhaps after you bathed and dressed . . . " He flashed a smile making warmth spread through her body. "Then my strength may return . . . for I am enjoying the view."

She gasped and then threw the comb at him.

With a laugh, and a groan he dodged her throw. He hobbled away. His wooden support thudded against the stone floor and then faded into the distance.

Kaireen flushed from the roots of her hair to her chest. She felt moisture between her legs. What was wrong with her? How could she hate someone so and then feel this way against her will. And she wanted her own bath, not leftover water that caressed him and still carried his scent of sea, mead, and musk.

The servant girl wobbled in, carrying a bucket of steaming water in each hand. At this rate it would be dark before the barrel was full enough for her to bathe.

Kaireen shook her head. Curse her for a fool. She would not love him. She would not.

Then Elva strode in carrying another two full buckets.

"Where have you been?" she screeched. "That heathen bathed before me again. And he had the impudence to suggest watching me as I bathed."

Elva ordered the servant girl to wait. Instead of apologizing, she folded her hands and then glanced back at her mistress. Nonchalant, as though to bait Kaireen's anger. "Last night you were intent on him living. Do you now wish me to have him die?"

"No." Kaireen flinched. "But he should stay in bed. Not wait around to catch glimpses of women trying to bathe."

"I had to clean and then rebind his wound with fresh linens."

"Why?" Kaireen flipped her hair back. "He could wash, and the linens be reused."

Six servants rushed forward, each carrying two buckets of steaming water. Then they emptied them into the empty bathing barrel. The steam played across the water like wispy fog.

"Silly girl." Elva ignored Kaireen's heated stare. "Clean linens will keep the fever away. Or as I asked afore, do you wish him ill now?"

It was easier to bide his presence when he was asleep. He looked more like a harmless boy than a Lochlann sea raider when he was unable to speak or hunt her down for kissing. Kaireen stuttered, but glanced away to compose her words. "No. But have a servant sent to my chambers if you are unable to meet your duties to me."

"Your water is ready. Did I forsake my duties?"

"I do not approve of your tardiness."

"Tardy or no," Elva sniffed. "I have your bath ready before this weed of a girl warmed two buckets." She nodded her head toward the servant girl. "Or does speed entice you so you wish to wash from a mere pail?"

"You take too many freedoms. See this does not happen again." She took the hazel twig the handmaiden offered, grateful that the flavor covered the tart hint from the drink Elva gave her last night.

After undressing, she climbed the wooden ladder into the bathing barrel. Along the edge lay a wool washcloth and a jar of soap. She scrubbed clean and washed her hair. Leaves, twigs, and dirt from her journey floated along the surface of the water.

Lately, Elva was too forthright. She would set her handmaid straight. Ensure Elva knew her place as servant, and she the mistress.

Kaireen scrambled from the bath with her mind set. Her body dripped water across the stone floor. She dried and then yanked on her leine. The material clung to her and her wet hair drenched her back.

She squeezed the excess water from her hair. Then she donned her gown. Panels of red left in the dye longer alternated with lighter shades.

Crossing the bathing area, Kaireen found the young servant girl in the corridor. She leaned against a wooden beam picking her nails.

Kaireen recalled not this servant's name; Marian or Leah?

When the girl saw Kaireen leaving, she snapped her hands to her side and fumbled into a curtsy.

"Have Elva waiting for me in my room." Kaireen waved her ahead.

"My lady, she already waits you there."

"How do you know this?" She frowned.

"She told me to stay here and wait until you bid me to fetch her." The girl reddened.

"Then make better use of yourself." Kaireen picked up her skirts. "Clean the baths."

Kaireen ignored her stomach rumbles and ran to her chamber. Her servant should do as her mistress bid her and not as she pleased.

As she pushed open her door, she ready to reprimand her handmaid, Elva interrupted her.

"Let me fix your hair." Inside waited Elva, ivory comb in hand and smile on her face. "You must speak with your lord father and mother about last night."

Kaireen faltered a step. Absently she smoothed her hand on the front of her dress. Her stomach flopped against her palm as she thought about what punishment they would give her.

"Aye." She swallowed. "Braid my hair, for I know not what they will require of me."

Elva beamed, guiding Kaireen like a child to her stool. The Laird O'Neill's sword leaned against her bedpost. No blood remained on the blade, so she guessed Elva had cleaned it.

Numb, she sat on the wooden stool. Not feeling the tangles eased at Elva's strokes.

Kaireen noticed Elva also had changed her bedcovers. Near the bed a fire fed on logs inside the hearth. The scent of pine filled the room.

All of the shutters along the outer wall were open. Sunlight and a cool breeze played across her damp hair, drying the strands.

Elva twisted her auburn locks into a braid. Then she secured the plait with a white ribbon. The end of the braid curled upward, brushing against Kaireen's waist.

"You are ready for them now," Elva said.

The fire popped and Kaireen jumped. Her stomach churned. Even though her father gave her anything she wished, his temper frightened everyone when it was unleashed. She had never experienced his displeasure for herself, but she had seen him cause a bishop to weep.

She scooted off the stool and then crept to the door. As her fingers grazed the handle, the door swung open. Kaireen shrieked.

Her mother's handmaid, Rhiannon, glared at her from the other side of the door. "Your lord father and mother request your presence immediately." Rhiannon's grey hair was yanked tight and forced into a bun at the top of her head. Her head covering allowed for no stray hairs to escape. At the sight of something, her eyes widened. Perhaps the view of the O'Neill sword made her pause. Her height was the same as Kaireen. But she had a way of staring down her pointed nose as though Kaireen was a spoiled child to be switched. "Follow me." She turned on her heel. Her heavy steps echoed through the corridor. Kaireen rushed forward. Once when she was seven, she had dawdled behind Rhiannon and was sent to bed without dinner for a week for her slowness. With each step her slippers hit the edge of Rhiannon's shadow. She rounded a corner as Rhiannon led her to the great hall. Servants scattered around to finish clearing the morning meal.

Her parents sat behind the high table, elevated by a wooden platform. Wooden trenchers were piled inside the kitchens' entrance. Her father leaned forward. Around the edges of his face, brown and grey hair curled. His green eyes, similar to Kaireen's, narrowed when he saw her.

A navy silk head-covering hid her mother's red-gold hair. She leaned back against her carved chair.

Rhiannon dipped into a bow, a smirk beneath her pointed nose. "My lord and lady, as you bid, here is your daughter, Kaireen."

"I know damn well she is my daughter," her father grunted.

Kaireen's mother shot a warning look at her husband. "Thank you, Rhiannon." She wiped a lace handkerchief across her brow. "Return to the dye-making quarters until I send for you again."

Kaireen heard Rhiannon inhale. But she curtsied and then left.

Bones, gristle, and squashed rushes littered the stone floor. In the corner a hound slept next to the hearth with his paw on his muzzle.

Kaireen smelled lamb stew and gooseberry pie. Despite her hunger, her stomach was tied in knots. The servants bustled around the kitchen, but kept their heads low.

Metal scraped against the cast iron pot, splashing water mingled with indistinguishable clangs and clatter from the kitchens.

Kaireen clasped her hands behind her. Her skirts concealed her shaky legs.

"Yestereve you were not present for the evening meal." Her father fingered his moustache, examining her. "Nor did you return from your land until well after nightfall."

She opened her mouth to answer, but his glare silenced her.

"Further, you arrived in tattered clothes, upon a stranger's horse and with no concern of our worries about what happened; you locked yourself in Bram's bedchamber for half the night."

"The door was unlocked, my lord. And two guards were outside the . . . ." She stopped at her father's ruddy face shift to purple.

"Until you are married, you are not to entertain him alone." His glare silenced her protest. "You have placed me and our family in a blood debt with the O'Neill's. You coaxed them into a dangerous battle. And gave my word, as if you were my bailiff instructed to act per my request." He slammed his fist against the table. "If I didn't know better, I'd think you the spy who has cost us a hoard of gold and men lately."

The hound jerked awake and looked towards them, then shifted into another position to sleep.

"My lord father." Her voice cracked for a moment as she struggled to steady her words. "Lochlanns attacked our lands. If I had not received help from the O'Neill's, then Bram and all of our own guards would have died. The Lochlanns would have raided deeper, perhaps reaching our hold here before they were discovered." She rushed on as her father shook his head. "Since the O'Neills fought with us, Bram and two of our guards lived. Given the chance, would we not welcome them as a choice for allies?"

Her father harrumphed. "Who we ally with is my concern, not yours."

Kaireen lifted her chin.

"I am the master and lord here. You disobeyed your future lord husband. Brought reproach upon my name."

His voice rose an octave and Kaireen doubted her knocking knees drowned out the sound. She remembered her father's treatment of enemies captured, or created.

Rivals were thrown into the pit. If they managed to dodge the sharp spikes, they were left to rot with rats and stone walls as their company.

Unless mercy and gold paid their passage to freedom, but often, her father demanded double the fee for the trouble of rescuing the prisoner from that pit.

She blinked, forcing away from the image of rats chewing the meat from her bones.

"I will have you trained as a good wife at least."

She had no wish to be a wife, but arguing the point with her father right now might grant her a night in the pit.

Sweat glistened on his forehead. He wiped the droplets away with his fingers. "Your mother and I have agreed on your punishment." He nodded to his wife.

Her mother smiled back at her husband and patted his arm. "First, you will go to the kitchens. The cook will give you bread, water, and whatever meat is available." Kaireen's mouth faded into a frown. "She has received instructions not to give you anything different. Nor set your tasks above anyone else. You will labor for her until after dinner is served and cleaned." Her mouth twitched on the sides. "You will assist the cook, and do everything she asks."

An annoyed gasp broke from Kaireen before she blinked. Her mother raised an eyebrow and Kaireen dipped into a quick curtsy.

"Work the kitchens until this same time two days hence. Then with Rhiannon on the dyes for three days."

Kaireen felt her skin pale.

"After which you will do penitence with Friar Connell for your sins. If he feels you have learned humility, then we will welcome you with open arms, and prepare you for your wedding feast."

At her punishment Kaireen's stomach flip-flopped, relieved for she would not see Bram while at the monastery. Friar Connell thought repentance mingled with strictness and labor did better than sorrowful words.

She squared her shoulders. So much the better, perhaps time and distance would rid Bram of this ridiculous notion that she would marry him. Perhaps he would fall for someone else more willing and suitable while she was gone. Or perhaps he would be discovered as the alleged spy.

In acquiesce, she stretched her skirts wide and curtsied. As she rose her father spoke.

"Break any of these rules, and your sentence triples."

As though seeing a devious glint in Kaireen's emerald eyes, her father chuckled. "No ideas now. You will marry Bram on the day agreed upon, regardless if you are covered in soot and grease." He laughed, as if the thought of her marrying looking like she lived in a pigsty was too vivid for him. He pulled his wife's hand to his lips and kissed her knuckle. "Now off with you, my patience leaves me."

Kaireen scuttled into the kitchens.

The cook was a plump lady whose jowls shook when she laughed. Her round face resembled dough with coals pressed in for eyes.

Her dark eyes did not flitter when Kaireen stood in front of her. She grunted, bending to remove a quarter of a loaf of bread from the ovens using her floured grey skirts.

She slapped the loaf on the wooden counter and then handed Kaireen a slab of pork.

"The meat is cold, and the old bread hard enough to break teeth." She poured Kaireen a goblet full of wine. "Get to eating with you; don't like slackers in my kitchens."

Kaireen thanked her for the food and bit a piece of the tough pork. The salted meat puckered her mouth, but she forced each bite. She gulped the wine and ate most of the bread and then threw the rest to the dogs.

This was not the quality of meal she was used to, but it was better than starving. After she drank another goblet of wine, she curtsied to the cook. "I am ready now."

The cook waddled to a mound of wooden trenchers.

"Scrub and rinse all of these. I do not want any stains or food left on them." Her coal eyes narrowed, examining Kaireen. "Not a mouthful for an ant."

Kaireen nodded, glaring at the stack.

The cook slapped her on the shoulder. "Wait 'til tonight. Me and the others already cleaned the rest of the dishes from the morning meal afore you stepped foot in the great hall." She toddled away on her spindle legs and shook her head. "When you finish, wash and peel the potatoes." She pointed to a sack in the corner. The mound looked huge to Kaireen.

"All of them?" she asked. The potatoes look as though they would feed half of Ireland.

"Should be enough for supper tonight. Now hurry girl. Still hands are lazy hands." Her laughter radiated through the kitchens.

After further instructions from the cook, Kaireen drew a fresh bucket of well water.

She scrubbed each trencher with lye soap until her eyes watered and her fingers burned, but she persisted. This was punishment enough. She worried that the lye would burn so far into her skin that her flesh would melt from her hands.

After eight buckets the trenchers were clean. Then she dipped them in buckets of fresh water. She rinsed her hands many times, but they continued to sting from the lye. Discarding the lye water into the dirt, she poured the potatoes in the buckets. After carrying them to the river and washing them, she hauled back the clean potatoes to the kitchens.

Back inside she snatched up a potato. She sat on a stool and then used a paring knife to cut away the skins. She wished she could cut away this arranged marriage and discard it like the ugly skins on the potatoes.

Her mind drifted to Bram. Did his wound heal properly? Would he have a scar? A blush crept up her neck thinking of his kiss again. His lips had been soft on hers, melting her resistance and penetrating her thoughts.

She griped about being a fool and raked the blade across the potato skin as if she might do the same with her traitorous heart.

Chapter Seven

A bustle of servants entered the kitchens surrounding the cook as she barked orders.

When she saw the mound of potatoes waiting for peeling, she shouted obscenities. Then she thrust the remaining heaps to two servants. "My lady's never done a lick of labor in her life. I should have known better than to think her to handle this."

The two servants bowed and then hurried to obey. They whispered and shot glares to Kaireen as slivers of potato skins flew around them.

The evening grew into mass chaos for Kaireen. Constantly she tripped and knocked things over.

When she turned the loaves of baking bread, three fell into the fire. An older servant sneered as smoke from the blackened bread choked the air.

The cook clamped her lips shut until the edges were whiter than the flour caked on strands of her dark hair. She smacked her palm with a wooden spoon then shoved the spoon at Kaireen. "See if you can manage to stir stew without burning it." She paraded to the doorway and then glanced at the guests who arrived in the great hall. "Good. Looks like thirty. Scrape the sides. Otherwise be a coat of burnt muck, hard to scrub off later."

Within minutes Kaireen's arm ached from stirring the stew. When her muscles seized, she switched arms. How could a servant's work be so draining when she had gone into battle against men, Lochlanns at that? Would her husband expect her to do all of this menial and exhausting work every time she displeased him?

The cook yelled orders and servants scurried to do her bidding. Some servants gave Kaireen a slight smile of pity. Others smirked as if she deserved her punishment or more.

After linen tablecloths were pressed, they were placed on the banquet tables. Knifes and cloth napkins positioned for each guest. A line of servants returned to the kitchens waiting instructions.

The cook inspected Kaireen's stew. "'Tis ready, thank the heavens." A trail of juice dripped down her double chin. "But you stirred the pot not like I told you." She laughed. "After tonight you will not make that mistake again." She turned back to the line of servants. "Everything's ready. No thanks to her." She waved an arm at Kaireen, who fumed silently. "Grab two trenchers each, fill them and take them to our guests."

The servants bowed their heads and then moved in rhythm.

Kaireen lifted the spoon and filled each trencher as the servants went by. Splashes of stew hit the stone floor. Globs of the liquid landed on the panels of her gown. At least the color matched.

After a while she did manage to fit a trencher with a spoonful, but it splashed onto the servant's livery. After the incident, the other servants held their trenchers at arm's length.

Bread, sausage, and ham completed the trenchers and carried to the guests. At last all of the trenchers rested on the tables and away from Kaireen. She doubted she would ever not appreciate another meal again.

With a frown, she plopped on the stone floor. Pieces of her hair loosened from her braid and brushed against her cheeks. She glanced at her hands. They looked like someone else's; cracked, swollen, and older. Her muscles ached for a massage.

The cook waddled to her on her stilt like legs. Kaireen smiled.

The cook did not smile back, but tapped her foot. "What do think you are doing?"

Kaireen glanced around puzzled. She had cleaned the trenchers, peeled a mound of potatoes, stirred this monstrous pot, and filled every trencher with the stew.

Cook did not wait for an answer. "Guests eat. Many will want more helpings."

Kaireen stared open-mouthed.

The cook pounded her other hand with her fist, making Kaireen cringe. "Get off your arse and keep stirring the stew. Fill the trenchers when they come back. Do not stop stirring until I tell you to." She glared at Kaireen until she did as told. The cook shuffled away, investigating another servant's progress.

Kaireen's arms were lead.

Soon the kitchens blurred with servants again. They rushed to refill pitchers of mead, wine, and trenchers with second and third helpings.

Kaireen gave her best glares to the cook's back. She could not afford to take any extra punishment for making faces at the woman. She focused on stirring the stew. But she imagined dumping the entire gooey mess on the cook's head.

A servant cleared her throat. Then Kaireen noticed the string of servants waiting with empty trenchers. "No time for dreaming," the servant simpered. "Fill or I tell your lord father and mother you sat on your arse all evening."

Kaireen smiled until her cheeks hurt. Inside she seethed. *Let us see how she likes cleaning the stables for a month.* At least, as soon as she was not punished anymore, Kaireen would find a way to pay this servant back.

Kaireen plopped a spoonful of the stew onto the trencher. Her smile froze in place in what she hoped was a mocking manner as the stew splattered across the girl's livery.

The servant screamed, but the cook dragged her away.

Her reward was that the cook waggled a finger at Kaireen, promising the distraught servant she would ensure Kaireen's added punishment for the mess.

She mumbled and continued serving. Soon she heard gasps from the other women, but she refused to look at them. She would not give these servants the satisfaction. She did not glance up when she placed another helping on the empty trencher before her.

"Our bairns will worry not about starving with your cooking." Bram's voice, filled with amusement, echoed through the kitchens.

From the shock she stepped backward, but he caught her arm, steadying her. She recovered and then wrenched her arm free. "I will poison your supper before we have any bairns," she promised.

"You wish to enjoy your time alone with me when we first wed?" He nodded at the other servant's crowding around. His fingers clasped her chin, guiding her to look at him. "If my loving is too much for you, and you want to enjoy me without bairns awhile, you only need say. No need for poison, my jealous wife."

In front of everyone he brushed his lips across hers, silencing her protest. He winked and then strolled away.

Kaireen threw the stew spoon at his head, but was too late. The spoon hit the stone arch and then clattered on the floor.

Her fist clenched as she strode to retrieve her weapon.

The cook's coal eyes glared from underneath heavy lids. "For your behavior this evening, you will clean the kitchens tonight—every trencher, knife, and pan . . . everything."

Kaireen tightened her grip on the spoon. The stew bubbled as she marched back to the kettle.

"Stir."

As she raked at the muck glued onto the cast iron sides, Kaireen willed the grime into everyone's stomach. With each pass of the spoon against the kettle set Kaireen's teeth on edge.

The cook nodded her approval.

Every muscle in her body cramped. She knuckled her back with her free hand to ease the tension. She waited for this day to end when she would be asleep in her bed.

The cook mumbled final orders.

"Pardon?"

"Feed the stew to the swine; it's been reused five times now." The cook waved her arm and her rolls of fat jiggled. "Then clean the pan until it sparkles in sunlight."

Kaireen nodded, and hoped she hid her glower. More days in the kitchens like this would have her begging for the pit.

She waited for the cook to leave, and then she dragged the kettle across the stone floor. The metal scraped an eerie sound as she struggled with the weight.

At the threshold, she anchored the back legs as she tugged the front forward. She tried to lift the kettle, but her arms did not reach around. The weight strained her until she thought her arms would fall off.

The kettle gave way and tumbled passed the doorway. Stew sloshed and she nearly screamed, seeing she would need to mop again.

Outside she huffed, pushing against the dirt and grass. For her trouble she stepped in a hole and lost her balance. She cursed and then snatched the kettle, smearing mud on her dress. The crescent moon hung high overhead. "I should have been asleep long ago," she complained.

An elderly manservant rushed to her aid. He helped her tip the kettle into the pigs' trough. His bald head glowed in the moonlight as he dragged the kettle with her back to the kitchens.

The leftover stew emptied, Kaireen bid him thanks. She dusted her hands, grimacing at the caked food and mud across her gown. She doubted soaking the burnt stew with lye would work to clean the kettle.

The servant bid her goodnight, and then huffed back outside.

Spying a metal spoon hung on the side of the hearth by a hook, she rolled her shoulders and then grabbed it. Glaring at the kettle as if it purposely caused her pain, she flopped down. With the spoon she raked the burnt stew from the kettle edges.

While she worked, she grew angrier that Bram had no punishment for yestereve.

Yet she was punished for saving him.

Chapter Eight

As he strolled down the hallway, Bram whistled. He hoped to lighten his mood with a song his father taught him on their sea journeys. The oak staff Elva gave him held well under his weight. His wound healed faster with her care then he would have believed.

He smiled at the thought of his future wife cooking and cleaning. He doubted she knew a carrot from a turnip. Aye, they would have strong warrior sons with her fiery temper.

Turning into the great hall, he saw a servant woman curled into a ball in the corner. Hearing her sobs bounce off the stone walls, he hobbled to her. "Are you unwell?"

She did not respond.

When he touched her shoulder, she shrieked. Her arms flew to cover her head.

Her brown eyes glanced at him and widened. She scrambled to her feet. And then brushed at imaginary dust on her livery for he saw nothing on the material. "Sorry, sir. I-I did not see you there."

He noticed the left side of her face was swollen and her lip cut. Blood dribbled from the wound.

"Who did this?" His anger boiled inside.

"N-none, sir." Tears welled in her eyes. "My clumsy feet flew from under me carrying the linens on stairs."

"Who did this?" He kept his voice low for fear the rage would seep in his tone and frighten her.

She whimpered, wringing her hands.

He waited for her reply. His eyes warned he would not leave her alone until he had his answer.

Before she opened her mouth, he knew the answer. "My lord husband." She seized his arm as he turned away. "But he means it not. Always he is sorry come morning."

"The one with dark hair and moustache? With ale glistening in his eyes?" He thought for a moment remembering the man's name. "Owen?"

Her silence answered him.

He nodded, but continued forward. Instinctively he knew which servant this was. Many men who beat their wives had the same temperament in front of others.

Smooth talkers, better at joke telling than others, and a sneaky evil crept through their eyes when they thought no one watched.

• • •

Half a side of blackened stew was removed when Kaireen needed to sneeze. She scooted back so her head would not bang against the side, like she did the first three times. Her sneeze sounded pitiful to her ears. Kaireen rubbed her nose with her forearm.

This was all Bram's fault. If he had not wanted to see the lands so soon. If he had ridden back with her to warn her father instead of insisting to stay and fight.

Climbing back inside the kettle she scoured the encrusted blackened stew.

Chapter Nine

Bram found a servant boy scuttling after a toad. "Where is Owen?" He knew the man's name and what he looked like by the battered woman telling him.

The boy stared at him dumbfounded, but then pointed to a man laughing with another in the hall.

"Tell him to come to my quarters now." Reaching in his coin purse, he placed a silver coin in the boy's hand.

The boy grinned, showing a broken front tooth. Coin tight in his fist, the boy raced down the hallway.

With the staff for support, Bram shuffled to his quarters.

Inside, he removed his belt and sword. He laid both across the stool, for he did not want the temptation now of his weapon.

Candles flickered, lighting the room. He was surprised Elva was not there waiting for him. She came every evening to apply fresh salve and linens, though he told her the old linens be fine. She ignored him, slapping his hands away, and did her work.

His room was narrow, but long. The hearth was small and he let the fire smolder on a log, but he liked the coolness of the nights. It reminded him of home in western Scandia. He wondered if Kaireen would like to visit his homeland sometime. No one would think it strange, like here, for him to practice sword fighting with Kaireen. Here Christian propriety got in the way of adventure.

He recalled when he first saw Kaireen. It was weeks before she knew he was there. Damn the vow he made to her mother, perhaps if he had not made it, things would be better between him and Kaireen.

His bed, with linens replaced, lay a foot from the back wall. Underneath the window in the room he had placed the stool. Next to the wooden shelf bolted along the wall faced the far side of the bed.

Another shelf cut across the wall to the right, a washing pitcher and bowl cluttered on one side with a hand towel draped over the ledge. Lit candles lined the other side.

Moments later a rap sounded. Bram stepped forward, leaning on the oak staff more than necessary. "Enter."

The servant man came in and bowed. "You need my services?"

"You are Owen?" Bram attempted to smile at the man's nod, but supposed it came across as a grimace. "Close the door, please."

The servant followed his orders. When he turned around he was then pinned against the wall with Bram's staff pressed to his neck.

"H-Have I offended you, sir?" His mouth quivered.

Bram twirled the staff, clipping the man under the chin. His eyes rolled to the back of his head. The servant lay in a heap on the floor.

Bram gripped the staff in his hands, his wrath wanting more. Instead, he took deep breaths to calm himself. Striking the stone floor with the staff eased the anger, some.

He had control again. He leaned on the staff and then hobbled to the shelf along the wall in front of his bed. He grasped the stone pitcher of water and carried the water back to the crumpled man across his floor. He doused the unconscious man with water, and he came to, sputtering and groaning. He rubbed his jaw, eyeing Bram warily.

Bram placed the empty pitcher on the floor away from the man's reach and then stepped forward.

The servant flinched.

"If you hurt another woman," he smiled, but knew his eyes spoke the truth of his fury, "I will finish you."

"You mistake me for someone else, my lord." Owen held out his hands.

"The serving wench," Bram ran a hand through his blond hair, wanting to ring this man's neck. "The one with cut lip and black eye? She is your wife?"

The man's pear-shaped face changed from shock to calm within moments. He grinned, but then took two steps back seeing Bram's blue glare. "I know where the mistake is now. Always she is clumsy. Yesterday, she fell down stairs. They can be unforgiving."

Bram grated his teeth. "Bruises like that do not come from stairs, they come from a fist." He took three strides forward. Concealed his pain with what he hoped was a snarl of anger.

He tapped the staff against his palm, staring into the other man's eyes. "Do you know of the blood eagle?"

"An e-eagle sir?" Sweat beaded across the other man's forehead.

"Many say 'tis a myth, but 'tis as real as both of us." The slapping of the staff echoed. "Many Norsemen refuse to tell a foreigner of how 'tis done." For effect he held the staff with both hands. Then dropped one hand, he whirled the staff straight and hit end against the stone floor.

The man jumped, his gaze locked on the staff.

"But I will tell you of the blood eagle, so you know I speak truth. The blood eagle is a slow death." Each word vibrated through the chamber. He wanted every word understood. "First, strap a man to a tree, his back exposed. Then the knife cuts him along here." He used his free hand to jerk quick motions along his back. "Then the ribs are broke open to reveal the lungs.

"With each breath you are in agony. With each breath your lungs cover in blood. Like an eagle's wings they flutter, until you die." He leaned forward. "Harm your wife, or any other woman," his stare locked into the other man's frightened eyes, "and I will carve you into a blood eagle."

Owen blubbered apologies.

But Bram glared at him and the servant snapped his mouth shut.

Then Elva swung open the door, a basket full of linens and medicinal herbs in her arms.

At the intrusion the servant crouched in a corner.

"Are you done with Owen, sir?" she asked sweetly.

Bram nodded leaning on the staff.

She held the door open as Owen crawled by. "And mind your manners. Lucky for you, your wife refused to allow Sir Bram to kill you this time." She closed the door and then faced her charge. "Well, off with your tunic. I do not have all night while you gape at me."

• • •

Kaireen's shoulders slumped as she continued to scrub the kettle. Her annoyance had long been replaced with anger gnawing at her stomach. Inside the kettle she sneezed; the sound echoed through her ears. She longed to crawl into her bed and never wake again.

She thought she heard a rhythmic thump in the distance. She ignored it. Probably it was the cook coming to give her another list of tasks to finish.

Kaireen quickened her pace scrubbing, so the woman would think she worked hard enough. But she doubted the cook ever got her hands dirty with cleaning or scrubbing this infuriating kettle.

At least Kaireen had finished all of the other chores, save this one. She had cleaned everything else. Her eyes and hands burned from the lye soap.

Now, this kettle refused to cooperate. She scraped the sides with the metal spoon. The handle engraved marks into her palms.

"Are you trying to make the pot sorry that it met you?" Bram said.

Kaireen jumped and banged her head against the side. Rubbing the back of her head, she eased out the rest of the way.

With a grin, he leaned forward, his hand outstretched.

She glared at him and scooted back.

Instead of arguing, he nodded. Then he balanced with the staff until he sat on the stone floor with her.

She smelled the aroma of Elva's healing herbs on him. Myrrh, hyssop, pine, and strong wine radiated through the air.

"I have work to do, sir. So if you please, take leave." The memory of his kiss angered her. She wiped her forehead with the back of her hand, smearing dried stew there. She saw his quick smile and huffed. "If you have come to laugh at me, then have your fill now and leave." She squared her shoulders refusing to budge.

"Why do I anger you so?" His voice was gentle.

Her thoughts drifted of her sister's laments of her husband who lingered into other women's bedchambers crawled through her mind. How would Bram be any different? His kind raped and pillaged for amusement. "Your affairs," the word tasted bitter on her tongue, "are no concern of mine. You may love whomever you wish. Only leave me alone and this ridiculous idea of us marrying."

"I will have you trust me if we are to marry."

"I will not marry you. I told you afore."

He ran his fingers through his blond hair. "I have always told you the truth." His dimple vanished when he frowned. "And I will forever do so."

She glanced away, but his fingers lifted her chin until their eyes met.

"I have no interest in any other woman." His thumb brushed across her lips. "Since you crossed my path."

She rolled her eyes, and jerked her head away from his touch.

"'Tis true." His voice sent shivers down her spine. "And you will feel the truth of my words." He leaned forward, and then caressed her lips with his.

She did not succumb to the heat spreading through her. Instead she clenched her fists.

His nibbling on her lips drove her to madness. She thought about punching him.

He pushed back and winked. "Our marriage night will chase away your lack of belief."

"I have told you, we will have no wedding or marriage." Perhaps she could get Rebecca to play proxy for her. She would have to convince them both that it was not by proxy afterwards.

She could run away. There were enough jewels in her possession to pay for a journey to Scotland and a small cottage with a few servants at least.

"Aye." He chuckled and used the staff to stand. "You will believe come the morning after." With a slight bow of his head, he turned to leave.

Her mouth worked but no sound came as he limped out of the kitchens. Aye, Bram was dangerous.

Chapter Ten

The Lochlann would cause trouble, Feoras thought as he cut the roasted duck on his trencher. The high table stretched before him, Bearach at his father's right hand, and he on his father's left.

His spy heard rumors in her circles with the Lady Liannon. The Lochlann rushed his men from across the seas to work on Kaireen's holding. They would arrive after the wedding feast.

No doubt, Feoras and his men must strike before this. Otherwise a score or more warriors would descend upon the O'Neill clan, swaying the battle in Bram's favor. The less men, especially Vikings, that the Liannon clan had on their side the better his outcome.

Battles never succeed exactly as planned. Feoras hoped to renew the bitter resentment of his clan against the Liannon's. Pity his father wanted peace and had worked so long to grasp its slippery garment.

Feoras' marrow boiled to rule both clans. His mother told him that although the younger son, he would accomplish great things.

Did not Jacob from the bible surpass his elder brother? She had asked when he questioned her. Would not Abel have the inheritance if he had slain his brother first?

Kaireen. How he hated the chit. This clan rejuvenation of unity was her fault. Women must be taught their place, lower than man and chattel, lower than slugs, which oozed from underneath his boots in the morning. Kaireen dared to fight with the men as though she were equal. She would be shown her place soon enough.

Resentment festered in his blood at the sight of her waving his father's sword at the Lochlann enemy. And the memory of her arrows shooting through the air turned his bowels.

He gulped his wine to quench his dry mouth. When he won the battle, he longed to smell her blood, in its pungent metallic aroma. Her defiant blood.

If he were given a moment alone with her after the battle days ago, she would have begged for death.

As though it were Kaireen in his hands, he tore pieces from the turkey leg. He stuffed the pieces in his mouth, his eyes rolling into his head at the pleasure of wishing this so.

For touching the weapons, he would rip her arms from their sockets. For speaking against him in front of his father he would carve out her tongue.

"Another leg of turkey, Feoras?" His father broke his concentration and he wrestled with not displaying his anger. "No father, 'tis enough for me here."

"We were wondering," Bearach added.

Always his brother had to contribute to anything his father said. As though he feared their father would forget his first born and allow Feoras to usurp his position. "We must compliment the cook, Feoras." He grinned. "For I have never seen you enjoy your food as much as now. But I have a liking for my meal as long as 'tis not alive." He patted his stomach and the others at the table laughed.

"We will see, brother," Feoras whispered during their joking. "Who is the victor of the battle."

"Wench!" Bearach bellowed, addressing their servant. "Tell the cook she has Feoras' heart through her cooking. Does she have need of a husband?"

"No." Feoras clenched his teeth. "She be too fair for me."

Men pounded their fists on the table. The serving wench laughed with them and then spun on her heel to the kitchens.

Moments later, the hunchbacked cook entered. Time and labor molded her back to its humped shape. Her blush was nauseating. She was thin, but her hands and feet swelled like they belonged to his brother and not a woman.

"Dance with her." The crowd cheered.

Tables scooted across the great hall, making room for the musicians and dancing.

He was in no mood for either. But his mother's words often filtered through his mind in times like these. "A laird must make his clan content, occasionally at his own expense. Do your duty once and they will remember you. Neglect it, and they will remember you not on the battlefield."

With a wink, he stood and then turned away from the high table. He approached the cook, and then offered his hand.

The cook reddened, but accepted his offer. Her hands felt as they looked, like greasy bloated meat. Instead of his grimace, he donned a grin.

As the musicians played, he swirled her round the room. Because of her bent back, her head met his stomach. For effect, he bent and then kissed her forehead. She swooned in his arms.

When the first song ended, the crowd whooped their approval. He should have ended it there. But he had not forgiven his brother's ridicule.

"Since this maid is so fair," he addressed the crowd. "All I have for her is . . . "

Baited, the crowd roared. But he waited until their attention was upon him again. The musicians ceased their playing. The men leaned forward to hear.

"I give her only what I can, another dance."

The music jerked into another song, and Feoras twirled the cook around the room.

"I fear they mock you and I," he whispered to her.

Never anger a cook, his mother had told him. For they might remove an offender with poisons, if they so choose.

"No worry." She smelled of pungent meat when she spoke. "Best time I have had since I was a young thing."

He nodded instead of commenting, because he doubted he could stomach another whiff of her breath.

At the end of the second song, she panted.

"At last fair maid." He swept into a bow. "You have put my dancing to shame with yours."

His brother and father were in conversation at the high table as though their interest in his affairs had already waned.

She giggled and curtsied back.

With a nod, he strutted away and then headed back to the high table. His plate and goblet were full. But eating now would keep him awake all night. He needed his strength for the upcoming battle with the Liannon clan.

Instead of eating, he tossed his turkey leg to the dogs. Then he swigged the wine in hopes his headache would ease.

How dare they mock him in front of everyone. Well, soon his father and brother would pay. Without a word, he bowed his head to his father. But his father did not respond. Infuriated, Feoras tugged on his wool cloak and then hiked to the gate tower.

Outside, his cloak caught the wind and billowed behind him. His boots hit the groove of the well-worn path to the gate tower. Days ago, his spy within the Liannon clan had sent word after seeing his father's sword in that abomination's hands. He climbed the tower steps, eager for the peace offered inside.

This was his refuge when his mother had been driven away. It was here he saw her face for the last time through the tower's south window.

Elias, his manservant, slept in this tower. Though missing his teeth and eyes, his ears heard the change of color on the autumn leaves.

When Feoras opened the wooden door, Elias snapped to attention. Before a word was spoken, he bowed.

"Leave me."

Elias jumped, apparently sensing his mood. In no need of prodding, he rushed away, closing the door behind him.

At last, Feoras was alone. His shoulders relaxed at hearing the bolt slide into place.

He moved to the window kicking, aside dusty bowls. Elias liked rats. Fed them from his hand. Filthy creatures, and they knew to hide when Feoras entered.

He gazed across the Irish landscape. Dusk had settled, casting the last golden glow on the oak, spruce, and ash trees. The whole land stretched before him as though in supplication before him.

His hands clenched. He missed his mother so, but she willed him to be strong. And so he would be.

Movement across one the rolling hills caught his eye. He backed from the window and rubbed his hands in anticipation. The spy's message was three days late; no doubt this would be great news for their battle.

The messenger bird fluttered through the open window of the tower. Around a leg, a fragment of parchment tied with a string. He opened his hand and the bird flew to him. It cooed as he stroked the grey and black feathers.

When the bird calmed, he worked at the knot round the leg. Frowning, for the knot twisted into more knots like a Celtic braid. Eagerness caused his hands to shake.

Whatever this said it was important, as his spy ensured the message would not fall from the journey. The writing would be in code, readable only to Feoras and his spy.

Elias left the bird and any messages alone. He knew the price of defiance, which was why he limped.

The bird danced on the stone floor shaking the tied leg.

"A moment more, little one." The knot gave way to a loop. Then he eased the bird's foot from the twine.

He unraveled the parchment then devoured the code. Thrice he read the words, and gooseflesh raced along his arms.

With this news, he would proceed with the plans for battle. With this, he planted the seed of revenge in his clan, and the blame swift to the foe.

His father's sword was in Kaireen's room. A meeting place was arranged for tomorrow evening.

However, diversions were necessary for his spy to steal the sword and meet him among the boulders to the west. She would not fail.

She promised. It would be good to see her again. Tomorrow could not come fast enough. And no one would know that he had his father's sword back. All would think it would still be with Kaireen. Perfect.

Feoras offered the messenger bird her cage. Elias would see to the bird's food and water. He tore the message into pieces and let them litter the stone floor. The rats would gather them for use in their nests.

It was a fitting end, rats to collect the Liannon clan's scraps. Feoras swept from the room. His cloak waved on the steps behind him.

The only lack was his father's death. His eyes watered at the thought. Not for mourning, but for eagerness. Everything he waited for was now in his grasp.

Instead of taking the path back to the keep, he strode to the stables. It was time to pay the witch a visit. She had failed in her duty these past weeks.

Aye, his father's sword would bring Feoras into battle at last. Bring him what the witch had not: good news.

Chapter Eleven

Kaireen slumped into her room. Muscles along her back, arms, and legs knotted while each step shot shards of pain through her legs and into her back. The back of her head burst open every time the heel of her leather shoe hit the stone floor.

She had forgotten her misery when Bram was near her. What magic did he possess to affect her so? Whatever it was, she did not like it. She would need to speak with Rebecca about him. It wouldn't take many words of encouragement to have her interested in him the way she gawked at him during the dance.

Tapestries lined the walls along the hallway. She brushed her hand across the weaves. Ages hardened the threads so the coarseness made her palms itch. Threads of gold, green, and blue colored the scenes. Red splashed through to mark a long ago battle between the O'Neill and Liannon clans.

Coolness of the night chilled her. She dragged her feet along, hoped the motion would ease the stabbing pain of walking to her chambers.

Her stomach rumbled and she could not remember if she had eaten. Little matter, she grew more weary than hungry. Never would she grumble about a meal again. She rounded the last corner, and then pushed open her oak door. In front of the hearth candles flickered in a circle. Fire chewed on cedar logs, filling the air with their scent.

In the middle of the room, steam danced across a large barrel. She closed the door behind her. Rubbed her eyes, and then looked again at the barrel.

It was wide enough for three people to lie in. Purple linen lined the edge, padding the barrel's rim. She shuffled closer. Her finger tips stretched to touch this dream.

Out of the shadows, Elva stepped, drawing her eyes to her. Kaireen jumped back, as if intruding on her handmaid's private ritual.

Elva tsked and strode forward. "Off with your clothes 'afore the water cools." Her fingers eased Kaireen's stew-stained gown off.

Then her shift and each of her leather shoes removed. All her coverings lay in a crumpled pile outside the circle of flames.

Elva led her to the barrel, and Kaireen stepped inside.

She slid beneath the water. The warmth and the lingering scent of honeysuckle caressed her. The bath massaged her skin, easing her soreness.

A sea sponge floated by her foot and she snatched the edge with her toes.

After washing her body and hair, she was amazed to find the water held her in a warm embrace for such a long time. Normally the water would be chilled by now. She settled lower. Her hair spilled along the back of the barrel. Purple lining padded her head from the sharp edge.

She heard Elva shake fresh sheets for her bed, but she closed her eyes, letting the bath lull her to sleep. Moments later her eyes flew open. The candles had been removed and snuffed. The logs, burnt to embers, lit her room. Her once warm water now stung with cold.

Elva stood before her with a towel. Kaireen eased out of the barrel and then grasped the towel from her handmaid.

She expected the pain when she placed her foot on the stone floor, but only coldness greeted her.

After drying, she allowed Elva to pull a clean shift over her.

Her teeth chattered as she made way to her bed. Climbing inside, Elva then tucked the sheets and coverlet to her chin.

"Elva?" She struggled to keep her eyes open. "Tell me why—about the barrel."

"'Tis a present," Elva answered her with a beam. "A present from me, child."

"Thank you." Kaireen yawned. Vaguely she wondered why her handmaid would gift her with a present for it was months past her birthday, or how she could afford something so costly.

She heard Elva's chuckles, but drifted away unable to open her eyes or respond. Her handmaid's laughing echoed in her skull.

Kaireen's heart beat faster at Elva's next words, but denial drove into her stomach. "When you and Bram use the bath together, I will accept your thanks then. 'Tis a wedding present; I suspect you will enjoy with your husband for many a time to come."

Chapter Twelve

Feoras was in good spirits. His spy had visited him in the woods, and she brought back his father's sword. She assured him that no one knew it was gone for now. He would need to be quick about the killing or it would be discovered missing in a few days unless a distraction was created. Like a fire.

Inside the witch's home, Feoras cracked his knuckles. He smirked at the crone who cowered before him. Her fist clutched her wool skirts as she backed further into the cottage.

In her clumsiness she knocked over a stool. Pity, she was the only one he knew in these parts. Others would squeal and use his visits to trap him. But he knew how to keep her from exposing him.

She reminded him of a wounded doe. Her sunken dark eyes darted about, as though in hope for a savior.

"Why is it not working?" he whispered and she cringed. He held back a smile. Whispers made imaginations run wild. She knew to fear his soft voice.

"M-my lord, I-I know not. The medicine should have done the course." She squeaked.

His fist hit the stone wall and she whimpered. "I am displeased." Blood seeped on his knuckles.

The fluid warmed his hand. Pleasure released through his body from the pain. Though his bleeding was not nearly as intoxicating as watching others bleed while squealing like stuck pigs.

Tears flowed on her gaunt cheeks. "Sorry, my lord. Give m-me another chance." She fell on her knees kissing his boots. "Please, I will make medicine . . . stronger medicine."

He seized her by her grey hair. Her face scrunched in pain. Never did he want to touch her flesh with his. Yet in his haste for his part of the battle, he had brought no weapons with him.

As if she saw his debate, hope sprung into her eyes. To answer her, he kicked her away.

In the corner, she cowered. Her wrinkled hands tried to shield her head.

He raked his fingers through his sandy hair. Leave it to a witch to call poison medicine. He cracked his neck to loosen the tension.

Maybe his father was blessed as a baby? No, she did not try hard enough. Do your best. The oath his mother taught him. Soon he would reunite with her.

His gaze fell on the baggy woman. Results are what counted, not effort. He would force her to do better.

She must try harder. So he snatched the witch from the dark shadows to persuade her.

Chapter Thirteen

Kaireen found Elva nowhere. She called for a servant girl to search for Elva in the kitchens, the great hall, and the courtyard. But the servant came back empty-handed. Desperate, she requested the servant to dress her. The girl tripped, dragging the yellow gown through rushes and dirt along the way. Kaireen gave the handmaid a forced smile.

Dusk and dinner would be within the hour. Nothing would ruin her evening. She had finished the kitchen chores on the morning meal, and now had the evening free before plunging ahead in the dyes.

Last night she dreamed of Bram. Of his kiss and that she could not get close enough to him. They had shared a bath together, then he laughed as she pulled rushes from her tangled hair. Why did she dream about him? Perhaps these hard labors had affected her mind.

She shifted her feet as the handmaid struggled to throw the gown over her head. Kaireen squatted to ease the girl's vain attempts.

Dressed, she thanked the girl. After she licked her fingertips, she rubbed them against the fabric. But the stains smeared rather than lessened. She saw the girl's tears welling in her eyes.

"No, 'tis fine. My clumsiness brushed me into a dirt wall if anyone questions." She touched the girl's nose. "'Tis not your fault my maid has lost herself."

Kaireen slipped on her leather shoes when her door flew open. The door struck against the stone wall with a boom, making Kaireen jump.

Elva stood before her hands on her hips as though upset at her mistress and not the other way around.

"Where have you been?" She held her arms to her sides to keep from shaking. How dare Elva barge in without apology?

"No time. Fetch the mistress her cloak." She snatched Kaireen by the arm and then dragged her along. "If you had waited a moment longer, I could have you better suited for the ride."

The young handmaid carried her pile-weave cloak, puffing as she chased them down the hall.

"Ride?" Kaireen stumbled. "No, the hour is late. Are you ill?"

"Wait too long and you will lose your way." Elva tugged her arm harder.

Kaireen skidded to a halt. "I demand as your mistress you explain yourself at once."

"Fire."

Kaireen paled. She sniffed the air, but only the scent of tonight's meal of roast chicken, ham, and onions answered. "I smell no smoke."

"Not here, my lady." Elva grabbed her cloak from the serving girl and then tossed it across her mistresses' shoulders. "At your sister Shay's."

Her hand flew to her mouth. She rushed forward, following Elva outside.

Men raced to ready their horses. Already mounted, Bram gave her a court nod. In the distance, fire lit the western sky. Her sister's home was on the edge of their land. It was about an hour's hard ride away.

"They will need every hand on this one." Elva said.

Kaireen opened her mouth to speak, but no sound arose.

Then Elva pushed her horse's reins in her hand. She noticed her horse had three blankets tied to the back of the saddle.

"To the fire." Bram led the men.

Kaireen mounted. Her sister and her niece were alone, she thought. Her sister would not be able to face another misfortune.

Already she had a difficult pregnancy. The child was due next month. Loss of her husband had nearly killed her. If she lost her daughter or the babe . . .

Kaireen shook her head and clicked her tongue to urge her mare ahead. They rode for miles. Flames glowed against the sunset. They heard the screams of their neighbors, heard the fire devouring the thatched roofs.

Kaireen halted her horse. Not caring that her skirts flew past her shins, she dismounted.

After she untied the blankets, she ran to soak them in the well. Fire and black smoke engulfed Shay's roof. Men and women filled buckets with water. Though they tossed the water onto the other burning homes, the fire hissed back at them.

Kaireen scanned the area for Bram, but saw no sign of him. The first blanket drenched, she tossed it to a man nearby. While she dunked another blanket into the well, Bram rushed forward to the fire as the first one to smother the flames.

Despite the night's breeze, Kaireen was sweating in her gown. Mixture of sweat and well water darkened the yellow cloth. Now she wished she had waited for her handmaid, she would have been dressed better for the ride and subduing these flames.

Fire popped sparks which hit the pine rafters of Shay's home. Kaireen heard a wail behind her. Holding the soaked blanket to her for protection, she whirled around. The wail was like the cross between a wind howl and a sound of a tortured soul who no longer knew it was dead.

On the outskirts of everyone battling the flames, Shay cried. Her sister sat rocking back and forth, her eyes riveted to the flames. She followed her sister's vision to the burning home, and a scream stuck in her throat.

Blackened by smoke, Bram stood in the doorway with a body draped across his arms. He stumbled forward, carrying the child. Steam rolled from the wet blanket covering them both.

Kaireen ran to him.

As she passed the crowd, she threw the wet blanket to open hands. Then she hiked up her skirts and sprinted to Bram.

Coughing shook his body. But he limped forward, her niece steady in his arms. Kaireen stopped before him. Unable to speak her disbelief of his actions and what she might say, she pursed her lips closed. No one ever entered a burning home. Those who did never made the journey out again.

Shay appeared beside her, and snatched her daughter from him. Megan was sobbing, but seemed fine.

"Thank you." She kissed her daughter's forehead and held her tight.

Bram shrugged. With an eyebrow raised, he watched Kaireen. Heat inflamed her face and she turned on her heel back to the well. Knowing he risked his life for her niece tugged at a piece of her heart. Part of her wanted to fall into his arms and kiss his foolish brave face. Then her resolved choked the notion away.

She dipped her third and last blanket into the water. Beside her Bram dunked his blanket in the well and it hissed from the heat of the fire. He sprinted toward the house to help the others dowse the flames.

Once again, she heard Shay's frantic shrieks.

She dropped the blanket when the words rang clear through the night.

"Douglas, my husband!" Shay cried. "Asleep, inside. Hurry, before the fire kills him."

"No." Kaireen waved her arms. And dread filled her until she thought she might collapse from the weight.

But Bram, covered in a soaked blanket, headed back inside the fire. He knew not Douglas was dead. Died months ago.

Clansmen and women stared at Shay. They knew the truth. Kaireen watched as he limped back inside.

Beside her sister, she skidded to a halt.

"Douglas!" her sister cried.

She grasped Shay's shoulders and shook her. Her niece clung to her mother's charred skirts. If Shay were not with child, Kaireen would have slapped her.

"He is dead." She fought the urge to slap her anyway when Shay broke into more wails. "You sent another man to his death looking for a ghost."

Did fate punish her? She had saved Bram's life once. Now, anguish knifed her heart. Her throat closed. Without thought she ran toward the burning cottage. Someone tossed a drenched blanket across her, but she did not stop.

Near the entrance, the heat coursed through her. Her feet did not stop as she raced ahead inside, bumping into Bram's back.

"What?"

A flame curtain fell behind them, sealing them in.

Now that she was here, panic seized her words.

The thatched roof had collapsed, blocking the doorway. There was no escape. If they stayed they would be cooked alive, only the blanket kept the sparks from licking her flesh.

Steam rose from the blanket in the heat. She realized if not for whoever tossed the soaked blanket her skin would melt like a beeswax candle. It was good that Bram already had a wet blanket when he rushed inside.

She had hoped to run inside the burning home and get Bram out. But with the fire hissing at them from the pieces of roof on the stone floor around them, she doubted they would survive. Soon the smoke would suffocate them and the fire would gnaw on their bones.

She shuddered. This was not how she wanted to die.

Chapter Fourteen

Black smoke poured through the rooms. Kaireen's eyes burned. Coughing wracked her and she slumped over. The weight of the doused blanket and the heat felled her to her knees.

"Kaireen?" Bram knelt beside her. "Are you mad, woman?"

"No." She hacked through coughs. "My sister is mistaken." Fire snapped the thatched roof. "Her husband died in battle."

"I realized no one was left too late." He heaved her to his side. "Now if you think perishing in fire will prove your love to me, I disagree. I will settle for you showing me with lovemaking on our wedding day."

She was about to protest, when crashing thunder answered. Fire burst through the roof and a piece of timber banged.

Shocked by the sound, Kaireen ducked. But the enflamed timber crashed down across her skirts.

Greedily, the fire scorched her clothing. Thank goodness her legs were not trapped. She needed to push the log off and she would be free.

But the log would not move. Heat pulsed through her hands.

Coughing beside her, Bram tried to move the log. "'Tis too heavy."

"Leave me here." She clenched her fist. It would do no good if he died because of her selfishness. She would have purgatory forever. "Others may come back with you to help."

He ignored her and patted the flames dancing along her skirts with his bare hands. Since he was stubborn, she hoped God would forgive her. Her hands ached as she too beat at the flames. With a grunt, Bram tore at her gown.

"'Tis my favorite."

"No one will care when the fire burn you and it to a pile of ashes."

Though she knew he was right, she could not keep the frown from her face. He ripped her skirts away and half of her shift. Wasting no time, she scrambled up.

No man had seen this much of her without clothing. She tugged on the remaining pieces of her shift to hide her legs from his sight.

As if not caring, Bram's hands thrust her forward into a back room. Smoke billowed around them, but she thought they entered the kitchen.

Shay's kitchen did not have any windows or doors to escape. They would die here.

Thoughts ran through her mind. If she ever got free of this mess, she would flay her sister until she knew the feel of burning from the inside of her bones and out. Kaireen's skin prickled in the heat.

Smoke burned her throat. With each breath, soot tickled her lungs. She doubted if she would be able to ever breathe without choking again, much less talk. Maybe this was her punishment for speaking her mind so much, instead of bowing to everyone as was expected.

Remembering the damp blanket she tried to cover Bram with the edge. But his hands shoved her forward. The blanket was dry from the heat anyway. His had long dried out as well.

• • •

Unable to see, Kaireen held one hand on the blanket and the other in front of her.

Bram shoved her forward. If not for her arm stretched in front of her like a sightless woman, she would have smacked her head against the stone wall.

"What is this?" she choked.

Perhaps she should have led them out. Bram had forced them both into the kitchen's hearth. The fire laughed at them from the doorway.

"There is no way out now."

"Let me handle this." His tone sounded harsh.

"Och, you have done a fine job now." She huffed when he backed into her.

"We are safer here than anywhere else inside."

"Ah, so when the fire traps us underneath the beams, we will die together then."

Thought she heard his teeth grate. "No, 'tis the hearth we are taking shelter in. Fire will not be able to burn these stones."

He was right, but the smoke crawling in did not lift her spirits.

She shifted the blanket to cover them. Her eyes caught the flicker of flames on the wood floor of the kitchen. "I cannot breathe."

"Cover your face with this." He handed back the blanket to her.

She shook her head, but his blackened face caused her to obey.

What was the use? They were trapped. They would die together, but at least she would not have to worry about marrying. The thought of her dying and Bram alive to marry Rebecca made her laugh.

"What?"

"Nothing. Thinking of what I shall do to my sister if we survive." She hunched inside the hearth with Bram's back facing the brunt of the fire. No doubt he wanted to keep the flames from her as long as possible. But the fire chewed at the wooden walls of the kitchen.

Through the smoke, she heard shouts, but they sounded so far away.

His body pressed closer to hers and she licked her cracked lips.

"Fire rages against us and the thing on your mind is a kiss?" His teeth gleamed white against his soot colored face.

"No, I wonder if I have the strength to push you into the fire for getting us here."

"Well," he winked. "'Tis not bad idea if you were thinking of kissing. Mayhap we need more practice if you cannot admit your thoughts freely to me yet."

She frowned, but already her lips tingled from the thought of his kiss.

With a coughed chuckle, he then leaned his head to her. His lips brushed hers as if she held nectar for him.

The thought of death lingered in her mind so she relaxed into his embrace. After all, if they died she would be forced to marry no one. Her lips opened for him with a sigh. Bravely she soothed her tongue across his. But he did not laugh at her attempts. His tongue danced with hers. Taken aback, she clung to his shoulders. Liquid heat melted her inside and it had nothing to do with the fire crackling around them.

He eased her hands from his shoulders and ended their kiss.

"Enough for now." He said between coughs. "The smoke will kill us soon."

When she opened her eyes, smoke engulfed the kitchen in darkness. She no longer saw his face and coughing racked her body.

"Lay down, the end will be soon." He whispered to her.

She obeyed, and was amazed she breathed a little better. Again, she thought of her torn dress and cursed. If Elva had warned her sooner about the fire, she would have donned riding clothes which would not be torn to shreds as they were now.

What if they died when the fire eased? All would see her dead with Bram and her legs exposed. It would be the talk of the keep for years.

Bram stumbled forward. His breath warm upon her face.

"Thought t-they would have s-soothed the f-fire by now." He sounded apologetic through his horse coughs echoed inside the hearth. "I guess I will not taste the warriors' banquet in Valhalla."

She ground her teeth. "Well, at least I do not have to worry about our wedding anymore."

"No need to worry even if we were not dying." He leaned his head on the stone floor. "You would have pleased me regardless of what you wore or did not wear to our bed on our wedding day. Though in case of another fire, I would advise against a gown sweeping along the floor as this one did."

She punched him in the shoulder and then worried she had broken the bones in her hand.

Smoke squeezed them. Until blackness settled over her and she could not breathe, could not think.

• • •

From a dark tunnel someone carried her. Her eyes were welded her eyes shut.

Voices argued around her. "The fire did not touch her skin too badly." A woman said.

"Did the fire burn her flesh?" She recognized the voice of one of the stable hands had fallen into a fire when he was a babe. His face was like a melted candle along one side.

Her hands bandaged, she scrubbed at her eyes to open them. Standing around her as she was sat on the ground was Elva, Shay, and some of the other women.

The fire of Shay's home was extinguished. But all that remained was the hearth and smoldering splinters. Fires mocked them from the other cottages and the field.

"Where is Bram?"

No one met her gaze. How could he abandon her like this? It was his fault for not listening to her when she tried to warn him.

Elva forced a vial of liquid in her bandaged hand.

"Drink this," she whispered. "Will ease the coughing and clear your lungs."

Though the liquid stung her throat, she did not weep.

Chapter Fifteen

Kaireen stared at the half moon creeping through the clouds. She heard coughing in the distance and people milling about.

Obviously she was ill-suited to have a husband. After her mourning, she would enlist in the convent. God must want her as a nun if disaster trod so fiercely on her heels. All of his bravery flooded back to her. He telling her to leave when the other Lochlanns came, whatever he said to Owen made the man stop beating his wife, putting up with her temper and harsh words, and even today fighting the fire valiantly to save them. The image of him covered in smoke and ash while he rescued her niece pulled at a piece inside her. She searched her mind for any noble men she knew who would have done as much as he and was chastened to know no one.

Fire eased its possession of the homes and fields as the men and women pounded the last traces with soaked blankets and cloaks.

Two chimneys toward above the wreckage like watchtowers. One was the one she and Bram had shared. Nothing stirred in the remains. She accepted the hugs of the women, feeling numb.

A man's hand wrapped in bandages and covered in soot extended to her. "Let the woman and child ride with you." The voice, tinted with familiarity in her mind, was clouded behind raspy coughs.

She nodded woodenly. Guilt made her look to thank the man for his help with the fire, when Bram's azure eyes held her. He smiled and his teeth lit his darkened face. She realized he held her hand, but while she wanted to keep holding on, pride made her jerk away.

"Someone must not want us dead." He winked.

Her handmaid pushed a colored flask into Bram's empty hand. "Drink this to rid your cough."

He downed the liquid and then handed back the flask. "Tastes like cedar and sand."

"Never mind." Elva waved her hand. "Sit and rest before you ride back."

"I am fine." He mumbled and then fell to his knees. "Well, maybe a rest will do me good."

Bram coughed three more times, then vomited black mucus. Then his coughing stopped. He breathed in and the muscles in his face relaxed. "Thank you."

Elva nodded and then stalked away to assist others.

Shivering from a gust of wind, Kaireen moved away to gather her sister and niece. Despite nearly dying, she could not keep a smile from her face. She mounted and waited for her sister to hand her Megan and then to mount as well. Her niece, Megan, sat before her in the saddle, her sister behind her.

Bram strode forward. "Take care." He scratched her mare behind the ears. "This fire did not rouse from natural causes."

She frowned at him. Megan whimpered against her.

He leaned forward, his hand brushing her knee. And she tried not to think about his hand on her bare skin. The fire had damaged this gown beyond repair and her shift did not give her much cover. "The hearth in the bedroom was the only one with logs."

"Perhaps a spark started the blaze upon the roof." Kaireen shrugged.

"No, the fire was strongest in the front of your sister's dwelling. The wind carried the flames sideways to the others. I wager this fire was created by the hand of an enemy."

Who would want to kill her sister? Her mind rummaged for answers, but found none save the spy.

"Take them to your father. We must offer them safety."

She opened her mouth to state she knew what needed done, when he whacked her mare's rump.

Chapter Sixteen

Rhiannon hung her mistress' gown on the edge of the window. A cloth covered the stone sill, allowing her to air the gown for tonight's supper and not dirty the material.

She fingered the velvet gown. It took her hours produce the color for her mistress. Glancing around her, she then snatched up the dress. Held the emerald material to her as if it was hers.

She sauntered to the polished bronze looking glass and admired her reflection. She did not see the lines on her face or the grey hair stretched tight into a bun underneath her head covering.

As if accepting a compliment, she bowed her head with a smile. She did not see her eyes grown cold from years of unhappiness and hatred. She returned the gown to the window. Longingly, she brushed her hands on the front of the gown. Velvet, soft like fur, but shorter. The color deepened as she stroked the material.

She stepped back. Her hand drew out the tattered envelope tied to the underside of her skirts. She kissed the broken seal. The seal of her clan, O'Neill.

Curse her husband Angus who sent her into the mist. So long she had waited.

Now in this letter she had her means of revenge, and the promise of enough gold to buy as many fancy gowns as she wished. Have her lord and lady kiss her feet.

For seventeen years she had been a servant here. When she arrived and told them of her plight, she wanted the Laird and Lady to rise up against her husband. The Laird refused and wanted her gone. His wife argued that it would be Christian to take her in.

He agreed, only if she would become a slave. Rhiannon refused and left. No other clan would take her in. Swallowing her pride for the moment, she returned to take her place as a member of the lower class. But she knew one day she would have her revenge on her husband and the Liannons.

She recognized Angus's sword when the child Kaireen returned. She had heard her mistress bemoan her reckless daughter many times, and Rhiannon had stoked the fire with her words to learn the details of the sword. Straightway, she sent a letter to the O'Neill keep—to the one family member who loved her, her son.

He shared her feelings regarding the laird, her husband. Rhiannon knew the laird did not know of his son's hatred toward him.

Hatred she helped to fester and grow in the child's mind. When Angus had discovered her secret, he had her banished, but only after his sons pleaded not to kill her.

"Never let him know how you truly feel about him," she had whispered to the young boy as she hugged him.

Angus thought he had remedied the problem. But it was too late, her roots had taken hold.

• • •

After Elva's treatment, Kaireen and Bram's hands were healed from the fire. Since their hands had been treated and bandaged in the dark, neither saw how much damage was done. Elva told them to keep the bandages on for a full day and then they could take them off. Her hands had been red and tender when she removed the bandages. Even the cook and servants felt pity for her as they did not require as much manual labor from her.

Kaireen was pleased with her progress today from the previous night of kitchen work and the fire. She finished her duties in the kitchens. She had made mistakes, but pleased the cook with her idea of adding onions to the stew.

After the meal the second night, a few of the servants stayed to help her clean. Her punishment was one-third done. The worst was yet to come.

Rhiannon.

She could not recall one instance of her acting nice. Rhiannon made lye soap feel like heaven.

Kaireen plodded down the corridor to the lowest level of the keep. Gossip flew around concerning Bram and some type of blood eagle. Rumors ranged from beating one with eagles, to letting eagles eat a person's flesh.

However, whatever it meant, the usual drunken manservant tonight did not have a drop of wine. He apologized to any woman he thought he may have bumped into. Sweat beaded his forehead and his eyes darted around as if the devil lurked to drag him away.

Kaireen smiled. She thought of Bram and his promise to always speak truth to her.

A blush swept over her as she remembered his other promises. Still, a part of her mind held a sliver of reluctance. Maybe this was a ruse as part of being a spy? Never had he given love as the reason for their marriage, only to obtain land.

Around the corner, Bram leaned against the wall.

Her breath caught in her throat. He wore a saffron tunic and hose. Cross gathers weaved round his legs and vanished into leather boots. His dimple made her flush. "I cannot stop thinking about you or our kisses." He strode toward her.

But her feet stuck to the floor.

He reached for her and her rebellious body softened in his embrace.

His lips lowered to hers and she threw her arms around his neck, deepening the kiss. What did it matter if they shared a few kisses? She still was not going to marry him anyway.

Aye, she remembered too well the feel of his lips upon hers. She did not care if anyone saw them. After the fire, she thought she might never see him again. She leaned into his arms; aware of the flutter in her chest which made her think she must have lost her breath or maybe the fire's remains had yet to be purged from her lungs.

Thoughts were lost in his embrace. It was as though she had drunk too much wine and could think of nothing but him. Her lips wanted the deeper caress of his tongue dancing with hers. Warmth spread from her stomach down between her legs. She could not get close enough to him. The touch of his muscled body soothed away the aches in her bones like the bath that Elva had drawn for her before the fire.

His tongue teased hers until they danced, becoming one rhythm. He eased away from her, breathing heavily. "'Tis best saved for our wedding day. No more, *ek elska pik,* my *ástir*."

She heard the Norse words, but did not understand their meaning. "Best to sate your needs elsewhere, for you will never have any lovemaking with me." She whispered.

"I've had a few mistresses before."

Her mind tormented her with images of his lips upon a buxom woman. She would not give him the satisfaction of knowing she cared at all.

"Leave me." She straightened. "I will arrange for father to pay you for your troubles."

"No." His tone made her step back. "I will not stray from our bed with another. This I vow upon the Norns."

She shook her head. "I will not marry you."

"Aye, you will marry me. You will meet my needs and I, yours. I promise you I will not stray from your bed."

Curse her. She knew men went through women like pigs rooting for truffles. Regardless if she had love in a marriage or not, she would not allow infidelity. "Pray you do not stray, for if you do I will shoot arrows into you and the wench together." The words were out of her mouth before she could stop them. She spun on her heel at his laughter.

Chapter Seventeen

Kaireen flipped her auburn hair back and took the narrow steps to the dyeing area.

Candlelight flickered across the stone walls. Though the sun rose and lit most of the keep, this part of the dungeon was devoid of natural light.

As a child, her mother explained the necessity of women dyeing here. If an invading clan tried to breech the walls, or dig underneath, then the liquid in the dye barrels would ripple and alert the women.

Until now, Kaireen had not visited the place again, because Rhiannon spent most of her time here.

Following the stairs round a corner, a stink crawled forward and choked her. Smell of sour milk, rotten swine slop, and urine. Rhiannon must be oblivious to the stench, because this aroma crept around her wherever she went. But here the odors clashed into each other, each fighting for dominance.

Kaireen wrestled with the urge to vomit, and wished she could race upstairs. Any punishment, days in the stocks, years in the kitchens, were better than this.

Now Bram would not want to come near her-which in her mind would be a good thing. Already she had become too used to his presence; she needed distance to strengthen her resolve not to kiss him again. She worried this brief exposure to the dyes may haunt her months to come. No, she was not a quitter. She would take her punishment.

To ease her nausea, she took breaths with her mouth. But she tasted the tingle of stink upon her tongue. She set her resolve and moved forward. Rhiannon would not be kind, especially if she was late.

Inside, barrels were filled with crushed berries, sap, onion skins, and various leaves crammed into every open space.

Wool and linen hung from the ceiling drying. Vats of colored liquid cluttered the floors. Torches lined the walls, sending flickering light across the massive room. Servants scurried about, applying sap to pre-dyed fabric. She watched while others stirred bolts of fabric into the vats. These quarters spread three times the size of her bedchamber.

Kaireen was amazed that none of these ladies appeared bothered by the stench. Many of them nodded their heads in greeting. Younger ones dipped into half a curtsy.

Within seconds Rhiannon snapped her fingers and then everyone jerked back to their duties. She strode forward, her gaze shifting down her nose at Kaireen. Her grey hair was tied into her usual tight bun. She wore a stout black gown which made her pale skin look like a shallow frame hiding bones.

"You are late. I will request your lord father and mother increase your punishment." She glared at Kaireen. "They have been too lenient on you. Long ago they should have sent you to the convent, or placed under my authority." Her dark eyes twinkled as if a secret existed somewhere in their depths.

Rhiannon strolled away and whistled for Kaireen to follow as though she called a dog. She pointed to the mordant barrels. These held alum, alder wood, and burnt seaweed. "These are applied to the fabric *before* placing it into the dye vats." Huge bolts of woven material of wool, linen, and others were piled high in sections.

Kaireen locked her arms to her sides in order not to strangle this woman. How dare she speak to her with an arrogant tone. "Why?" she asked with as much loathing as she dared.

"Why?" Rhiannon looked back at her with an eyebrow raised. "To help the dye stay on the material, of course. Then the fabric is cut and sewn into garments."

With giggles echoing from some of the women, she then pointed out the dyes of the room: vats of nettle for green and brown colors. Saffron for golds, silver birch for browns, onion skins for oranges or browns, and woad for blues.

Rhiannon stopped between a vat of crushed privet berries and a barrel of alum.

"Take that bolt there." She pointed to a stack of linen and wool. "Rub every inch of it with this alum and salt. Rachel?"

At her word, a plump girl with yellow braids waddled forward, carrying a cup full of salt. Rhiannon rolled her eyes at the servant's clumsy curtsy, which nearly toppled the girl on her face.

"Let them set with the mordant for an hour. You may help the others while you wait. Cook will send food by noon. Plunge the bolt in the privet berries, and stir so the color distributes equally." She stomped away.

Kaireen wrinkled her nose and picked a length of wool. She used her hands to spread the alum mixed with salt. The sticky alum with gritty salt stuck underneath her nails. Soon her palms were raw from scrubbing.

Rachel, who brought the salt, gestured with her chubby hands how to spread the mixture evenly. Red colored her cheeks as she grinned at Kaireen's words of thanks.

Rhiannon paraded around, shouting orders and insults at the other workers. Never did she insult Kaireen, but she held her assaults on the tip of her tongue. Her tone cutting her words as if slapping. "I do not think you have the skill for this, Kaireen. We will be happy to have passed your last hour with us."

At noon, Kaireen bit a piece of meat from a chicken leg. After cleaning her hands three times, she felt as though she still had salt underneath her nails.

Through the fabrics scattered across the quarters, she glared at Rhiannon. She smiled at the vision of dunking the woman into the foul smelling vat of woad.

After they finished eating, everyone went back to their chores. Kaireen assisted Rachel to smear burnt seaweed onto a wool mound of wool as preparation for the dye.

Soon, her bolts would be ready to dye. She bent her head to tell the young girl goodbye, when Rhiannon bellowed her name.

She cringed, but then schooled her face. "Aye?" She stopped at the woman's glare.

"What are you doing?" She looked as if she had eaten an old egg. "'Tis past time you dyed your pile of fabric instead of talking."

Snickering rose from the corners of the room. But when Rhiannon looked, with a smile, none of the servants gave any clue as to who had laughed. Her smile faltered as she glared back at Kaireen. "No doubt you're spreading your empty headedness with talk of jewels and spoiled pampering."

She clenched her fists. Rhiannon watched her, waited for her to err, and humiliate her for it. She bent, gathering the sticky fabric and then dumping them into the vat.

Kaireen grabbed the long handle of a paddle, hitting the sides of the vat as she stirred the liquid.

She forced the fabric down, not allowing them to float to the surface. She would show Rhiannon. Hers would color better than anyone's.

Half an hour later, women crept by, murmuring to Kaireen that the dye was done. But she refused to listen, her green eyes locked on the grey bun yards in front of her.

Her arms were numb from stirring, but she would not stop. She would not give the woman the satisfaction of her failure. If a few minutes were called for to soak the linen, then more time would make the color better, she reasoned.

Evening approached and Rhiannon examined each of their work. She stopped at her vat and tsked. "My, my." She held her hand for the oar.

Kaireen handed it to her. Though Rhiannon smiled, her smile sent shivers down Kaireen's spine.

"This will not do. You need to smear oak galls into this now. I am afraid this will take you into the night until you may go."

"Wha—why?" Kaireen stuttered. Her face flushed red.

"Oak galls dull the color. No one will want to wear this bright uneven color when this dries." She held the soaking fabric of a splotching purplish blue and the others laughed. "Looks like dumb peasant work. Now, Rachel will give you directions. Try to follow them correctly this time." Rhiannon snickered as she sauntered away.

Laughter echoed as she climbed the stairs with the others following after her.

Kaireen grasped the drenched fabric and tried to hurl it across the room. She was aiming at the far wall, but it was too heavy and sloshed on the stone floor instead.

"That will leave a stain." Rachel twisted one of her blond braids. She bit her lip as if concerned she would take the punishment for it.

"I will tell Rhiannon the truth. The spot was from my hand." Her fingertip of her clean hand touched the girl's freckled nose.

Chapter Eighteen

Sunset on Kaireen's last day with Rhiannon and nothing the woman said or did could affect her mood. Her punishment was nearly done.

The stench did not smell as strong as her first day. However, she begged Elva for herbs to take away the smell upon her skin and hair. It was as if Rhiannon haunted her with the stench of her work sticking to her skin like the vats of dye.

Supper with guests gagging around her proved embarrassing. Kaireen protested she had taken two baths, but nevertheless, was ordered to her quarters to eat her meal.

Rachel, though a young girl, taught Kaireen enough of the important rules to avoid any further major mistakes. The oak galls worked on the first garments she had dyed. Now the color was no longer patchy or blinding. After she wrung out a swath of linen, she hung it across one of the lines for drying. Since the garment was still ill suited for a noble, Kaireen had asked to keep it. Elva could sew the material into something useful and it would be a reminder to Kaireen how hard she had worked.

Rhiannon left for the moment to tend to her mistress' call.

Everyone relaxed after she had gone. Laughter echoed among the women working with the woad dye.

Kaireen hummed a tune. The song she and Bram had first danced to. When she realized which song it was, she switched to another. With the back of her hand she wiped sweat off her brow. Thankfully Bram would not want to hold her close since she smelled like rotten fruit.

Rachel sat half-way up the stairs, twirling one of her blond braids. She was the lookout for everyone. If Rhiannon opened the creaking wood door, everyone would grow silent, working.

Rachel gasped jumping from the stone steps. "She comes."

A woman in the middle of a song about a man with rubies on his fingers snapped her mouth shut. Ladies who danced now rushed back to their vats to check the consistency or soak their bolts of fabric in their mordant.

The footsteps on the stairs clanged through the chambers like distant church bells warned of impending disaster.

Across from her, a woman managed a weak smile. Her long face stretched forward as if her ears burned to hear.

On the stairs a man coughed and the women screamed.

"Rachel, see who comes." Kaireen shifted her weight. Why did a man coming frighten the others?

Whispers rose as Rachel scampered to the stairs. Moments later she came running back. "'Tis Bram. He has come looking for you."

Women crowded around her.

"You must stop him." The woman with the elongated face squeezed her arm. "Take him back upstairs."

Kaireen pried her fingers off and then smoothed her grey skirts.

"Why should I? The stench alone would keep anyone at bay not forced to endure this."

Rachel spoke wringing her hands. "If a man comes anywhere around the dyes, it ruins them." Her eyes watered. "Rhiannon will punish all of us for this."

"Ruin the dyes?" Kaireen glanced around her and the others nodded their heads. "Nonsense." But she saw fear in their eyes.

They stepped away from her, mumbling.

Kaireen waited with her hands on her hips. The footsteps on the stairs sounded louder.

The throng of women rushed her at once. They whirled her around and then pushed her to the stairs.

"Let me be." Kaireen struggled against them, but there were too many.

Round the bend, she saw Bram's shadow. Despite the obscurity of their fears, she would not allow them to humiliate her in front of him. The thought of debasement sent knots into her stomach.

"All right. I will go and make him leave. Let go of me."

The women obeyed. Some descended back down, but a few remained with their arms crossed.

Kaireen raced the stairs. Finding Bram, she clutched his hand and tugged.

But he stood there with a grin on his face. The dimple in his cheek was so strong she wanted to kiss it. Blast it, she needed more time away from him to rid herself of thoughts of kissing him.

Instead, she brushed a strand of her auburn hair from her face. "Why are you standing there?"

"I missed you." His blue eyes shimmered.

"Miss someone else. You need to get away from here." She jerked on his hand, but he would not budge. Then he grasped her around the waist, hauling her to him.

She bit her lip knowing what she must smell like and yet he was still undeterred. One hand held her to him, the other stroked her hair. She felt the heat of him throughout her body.

"Has your wound festered?" she asked, attempting to distract him. "I will tell Elva you need more salve."

He brushed his lips across hers, making every vat and mordant vanish leaving only his smell of leather, sea and the hint of mead on his breath filling her senses. His tongue wet her lips, sending shivers down through her fingertips.

His kiss became hungrier, more intense as she opened for him. Their tongues stroked each other's. Kaireen's hands grasped his hair.

Bram smiled against her lips. Then he pulled away from her. Their gasping breaths appeared like wisps of white smoke between them.

Pretending as though nothing out of the ordinary had happened, she brushed her grey skirts. She hoped her shaking legs would not give away how he made her want to rip his clothes and feel his skin beneath her fingers.

She felt Bram's stare. He leaned against the wall, the grin bigger than before.

"What?" She placed her hands on her hips.

"Your kiss speaks more to me than your words." He winked at her gasp.

"Sir, you take far too many liberties." Rebellious to her mind, her heart thumped inside her chest, echoing through her body.

He tilted his head to the side. Oh lord, did he hear it too?

"Mmm." The deep vibration of his voice sent wetness to her loins. "I have taken too many liberties with you."

She stared at him opened mouthed.

He chuckled, "I do not know what possessed me to think I could wait a fortnight to be with you."

"I think it's best that we cease kissing or anything else. I am not a wanton and since I will not be married to you, I won't be seduced by your lips or body any longer." Wanting to kiss him had lodged deep inside her and was spreading like a sickness. Time she lanced it out. She climbed the stairs. It would be agonizing, but it was better now than later.

She did not hear Bram's footsteps behind her.

"Well?" She spun around and saw Bram was where she had left him.

"Here I stand, waiting for you to admit the truth as your heart feels it." He looked at her.

"Admit what? That you are an arrogant fool?"

"Tell me you have missed me too." His tone grew serious. "Say the words, or we will stay here all night."

"Did you not hear what I said?"

"I heard a lie that you want to be truth." He leaned against the wall studying her. "Why is it so hard for you just to admit you have a fondness for me, no matter how small?"

She wiped her hands on her wool dress. Sweat trickled down her back. Normally, she would let him stay there all night. However, the likelihood of Rhiannon returning increased with each moment.

She could not risk further punishment for herself or the other servants. Already she fantasized about holding Rhiannon's head in a vat of woad until her eyelashes and teeth turned blue. If Rhiannon found him here and vented her anger on them all, Kaireen may not be able to smother her own fiery temper any longer.

No doubt she would have to give her penance for those thoughts with Friar Connell. She clenched her fist and straightened her back. "I may have missed you like a cat misses a flea." She snapped. The admittance of her heart loving him angered her. Why should she be the one to fall in love? Why could she not stop before she fell too far?

The muscle in his square jaw twitched.

She caught his intent as it crossed his face and she backed away. "No, nothing more."

In two strides he barreled down on her. His arms locked her in place. "Admit you long for me as I do for you." His breath nuzzled her neck.

She lost her balance, but clutched his arms. "I told you, we will have no wedding." She lifted her chin.

"At least admit you long for me." He kissed her neck, then the line of her jaw. "We will not leave until you do." As if he noticed her hesitation. "I think Rhiannon is nearly done with your mother's dressing."

She looked over her shoulder, half expecting the wooden door at the top to creak open at his words.

"Fine." She glanced back into his blue eyes smoldering with the hint of more than kisses. "I long for you to be gone."

He frowned, but then stroked the golden stubble on his chin. "I'll take the first of your words as a beginning." He let her lead him to the stairs.

At the top, she opened the door a crack to see. No sign of Rhiannon. Shoving him past the door, she then pulled the door closed behind them. It was like trying to move a boulder that even the wildest storm could not budge.

Kaireen leaned against the door. Bram kissed the tip of her nose.

"I know how you feel." The dimple appeared in his cheek again. "I am as breathless as you." his dimple twitched, "because I cannot wait for the day of our wedding dance either."

He strutted away chuckling. Chasing after him, she hiked her skirts out of her way.

Chapter Nineteen

It was past dark when Kaireen and Rachel nearly finished their chores. She worried the girl would not be able to stay standing for much longer.

"To bed with you." She shooed her up the stairs. "Thank you for your help. But I can sweep the floors alone."

Rachel answered her in a yawn and then climbed the stairs.

With a huff, Kaireen grabbed the broom. She had been here too long. The stench she smelled upon first arriving did not seem so strong. Still it was as if Rhiannon's presence stalked her everywhere.

She was in middle of sweeping when the door at the top of the stairs banged open.

The sound made her jump.

Did Rachel stumble through the door?

"Kaireen." It was Bram. Just her luck, Rhiannon may come back and have her work all night because of his intrusion.

What now? Did he not have enough time earlier to baffle her? She threw the broom down determined not to let him embrace her. She would be resilient.

They met on the stairs. When he did not make a move for her, she bit down the disappointment that he did not take her into his arms. Hadn't she said she wanted him to stop? Why did she feel distraught that he might obey?

"Have you seen Elva?"

Is this what he bothered her for, her handmaid's whereabouts? "No, have not seen her for some time. She and Rhiannon dislike one another, so Elva doesn't come to the dye chambers if she can avoid it. Not to mention the stench."

His eyes grew dark, and Kaireen wished to take the bite out of her words. "'Tis your sister, Shay. The babe comes too early."

No longer caring about Rhiannon and the punishment she would receive for leaving her chores unfinished, Kaireen pushed past him to the stairs.

• • •

Inside the bedchamber, her sister lay pale and dripping with sweat. Pain radiated through her face as Kaireen rushed to her side. The midwife shook her head when Kaireen glanced at her.

Her mother wiped Shay's brow.

"Douglas always wanted a son," she grunted.

"Aye, but he would want you both healthy," her mother added.

Muscles in her face cramped and she screamed. The sound grated across Kaireen's bones. Never did she want to have a child now.

Still the babe would not be born, nor did Shay's pains ease.

"'Tis too much for her. I fear she and the babe will pass," the midwife whispered.

"No!" Shay screamed as another spasm tore through her body. "My son is strong and ready."

"When did you feel the babe kick last?" the midwife asked.

Shay did not answer, but tears streamed down her face.

Silence choked the air. None spoke, but continued to help Shay push the child from her womb. An hour passed before each stared at Shay's son.

The cord was wrapped around his neck. His blue skin showed he did not breathe. The midwife eased the cord from his neck.

"Let me hold my son."

The midwife did not answer her, but rubbed the babe's arms and legs as if to wake him.

"Give me my son."

With a sob, the midwife placed the lifeless child in Shay's arms. "Sorry milady, but he did not make the journey."

Shay cooed to the child as if he were alive. "See, he has his father's chin."

Kaireen cried. It was unfair the suffering her sister had to endure. She wished to take the burden of her pain away.

"Let us clean him for the burial," her mother soothed.

"He is all I have left of my Douglas. You will not take him."

"What of Megan?" Kaireen asked, but she was answered with a scowl.

They let her cuddle and speak to her son while the midwife urged the afterbirth out, and then cleaned the birthing.

"Shay." Her mother brushed back her daughter's blond hair. "Let him go. Douglas waits to greet his son, too."

With words of encouragement, Shay let the midwife take her son. She sat watching them leave.

Then she rocked back and forth in the bed, singing a child's song of mourning.

"I will wait with her tonight," Kaireen said dragging a stool beside the bed.

Her mother and the midwife nodded and then left.

Kaireen dug through her sister's old trunk and removed a fresh leine. Then she eased off Shay's sweaty leine.

Using the water from the pitcher and a rag, she cleaned her sister, and then dried her. Then she dressed her sister in the clean leine.

She chatted about her punishment and the smell of the dyes. But her sister did not answer her. With the bed linens changed, Shay lay upon the bed.

"Come the morn, you will have a proper bath. The warm water will sooth you."

Unsure about what else to do, Kaireen blew out the candles, and then climbed into bed beside her sister. Waited until she heard her sister breathing before she let sleep take her too.

...

Sunlight crept through the window. Kaireen stirred, disoriented that she was not in her room.

Then she remembered. "Shay?"

Her sister did not answer her. An eerie silence waited. She hopped from bed and then rushed into the hallway. Perhaps her sister bathed this morning. But her heart knew otherwise.

A servant scrambled down the hallway.

"Have you seen my sister?"

"No, miss."

Kaireen rushed to her parent's chambers. Outside their door, she pounded on the wood.

Her mother swung open the door.

"Have you seen Shay?" she asked before her mother spoke.

Moments later, everyone searched the keep for her.

But she could not be found.

Kaireen hitched up her skirts and raced to the stables. The stable boy confirmed her fears, that two horses were taken in the early morning. She knew Shay had taken one of the horses, but who had taken the second? She could not dwell on questions, so instead saddled her horse, and then mounted. Outside, she galloped to the coast. And she prayed she was not too late. She should have stayed awake all night. Let someone else watch her sister after the morning meal.

After hours of riding, she passed the hill before her own keep.

One of the missing horses grazed ahead. Instead of stopping to catch the beast, she rode on.

At the edge of her keep, the other horse skirted away at her approach. She saw a figure hunched at the edge of the cliffs. After her horse halted, she jumped off. Her bare feet flew across the grass.

Now she realized she did not put her slippers on this morning. As she was breaths from the figure, she realized it was Bram. His wool cloak covered his frame.

She heard his remorseful voice mixed with the waves crashing against the sea. Her heart leapt in her throat. He cradled Shay in his arms.

Chapter Twenty

Kaireen forced one foot in front of the other as she stalked around him.

As his hand brushed Shay's hair, he stared at the waves. "Did not reach her in time."

At his words, Kaireen wanted to shout for him to stop. She could hear no more.

"The babe slipped from me as I snatched her back." His shoulders shook and Kaireen heard the dismay in his voice. "I did not know about the babe . . . knew not she had him with her."

"The babe was already dead." She saw his shoulders relax and she moved beside him. Her heart jerked at his compassion and the risk of his own life to save another once again. But why would this affect her so? He'd done as much at Shay's fire. Maybe it was because his choice to do so, and he did it without expecting a reward save their marriage.

She heard Shay groan. "She lives?"

"Aye. But only on the outside."

Her sister stared back at her with hollow eyes. "Douglas calls me to him."

"No, Douglas—" What could she say? Her sister would not listen. It was only a matter of time before her sister wasted away or succeeded in her breaking her body upon the rocks.

"Let us get her back to your father's keep." Bram stood. As he carried her sister, she rounded up the other horses. They tied Shay's mount to his. But let Shay ride alone with Bram's horse leading hers. Mounted, they rode back to her parent's keep.

"Perhaps after a few days, she will be better," he said as Kaireen nudged her horse closer to his.

It was a miracle he was able to hold onto her sister. She was more like Kaireen than anyone else. And she knew, if she had her heart broken twice, no one would have been able to snatch her from death as Bram had done. "Did you chase after her here?"

"I was already here at your keep."

"How? Why?"

"'Tis my wedding present to you." He winked at her.

"No need, we will not have a wedding as I have told you 'afore." When would the daft man listen?

He did not answer her, but let their horses guide them back.

• • •

Inside Shay's room, her sister squatted in a corner, refusing comfort or food.

Her blond hair was matted, and the smell of the birthing from last night clung to her.

"Shay, please." Kaireen reached for her. "Megan worries about you. She's too young to understand."

But her sister did not answer her. Only sang a baby's lullaby.

"Let us bathe." She held out her hand and tried to smile. "Who will watch your daughter if you go?"

Her sister's song ended in mid-sentence. "Father and Mother." She waved her hand as if shooing a fly. "Or you and your husband."

"I am not married," Kaireen huffed.

The hint of a smile crossed Shay's features for a second, and then disappeared.

What else could she say? Her mother and father cared for Megan. The child, almost three years old, did not understand why her mother did not come to the morning nor evening meals.

Already, the sun dipped to the west. Bram had been no use since they returned. After caring for his horse, he had wondered around outside.

"At least eat something," Kaireen begged.

Her sister resumed her rocking.

Then a knock sounded on the door as though whoever it was held good news instead of the tragedy her sister bore.

Elva entered with a smile. "Out of bed with you, lass. Time for bathing before the meal."

"My Douglas and son call to me," she moaned.

"Do not speak nonsense," Elva chided her. "No excuse got you out of a bath when you were Megan's age, and it will not now."

"She has suffered—" Kaireen objected.

"Only prolonged by herself." Her handmaid looked at her so intently that Kaireen took a step back. "Now, rise or I will lop off your hair."

Her sister did not respond.

"You want to be bald when you meet your new husband?"

What was Elva speaking of? Already her sister had lost her husband in death, she did not need another.

"Douglas was my love. I will have no other."

"Aye, but you have been blessed."

"Blessed?" Kaireen screeched. How could her handmaid be so crude?

"If you are finished, or do you want more trouble from me." Her handmaid squeezed her hand as though telling Kaireen to keep her mouth closed. "Then I will turn a switch on you myself as your mother so often threatens to do, but never has."

Kaireen frowned, but nodded. What would her ramblings hurt?

"But I cannot marry. Douglas was my only love."

"You are blessed, because great love will come twice in your life."

Shay glared at her.

"'Tis truth I speak. Did I steer you wrong about Douglas?" Elva waited a moment, and then rocked back on her heels. "Now, then, do you want the first memory of you for your new husband to be like this?"

"I lost my love." She shook her head. "I will not marry again."

Elva yanked Shay by her hair. Kaireen screamed and pulled her handmaid's arms. "Aye, Douglas was your night."

At her words, Shay's arms fell to her sides.

"But this one will be your day." She released Shay and held out her hand.

Her sister took it. They strolled down the corridor, to the bathing room.

Kaireen followed them. She would not let her sister drown herself in the bath.

"Where is he?" Shay whispered as if this false husband would leap from the stone walls.

"He comes from across the sea."

"I get seasick."

Elva patted her hand as they walked. "A giant of a man. You will tame his tongue to our language, and he will tame your stomach for the sea."

"But what about my son? Why did he have to die?"

Not looking where she stepped, Kaireen tripped. What would her handmaid say now?

"Was not his time to come yet."

Tears welled in Shay's eyes, and Kaireen feared the singing again.

"Yet, the wheel turns right again for you. Your son will return, but he will bring four brothers with him."

Kaireen shook her head. It was not right for her handmaid to fill her sister's head with fancies that would not come.

"Each will be born on the sea. One during a storm."

Inside, Shay undressed. Then she climbed into a steaming tub. "Join me?" she said to Kaireen.

A bath did sound pleasant. She had not bathed since yesterday morning and knew she smelled of the dyes.

"Please, sister," Shay said. "You smell worse than manure."

They laughed.

"One moment." Elva spoke and took Kaireen's arm. Her handmaid escorted her away from Shay's hearing. "Do not undo my work."

"Your work? You mean your ramblings?" She hugged her arms across her stomach. "What happens when this does not come to be?"

"Mark my words, if you throw doubt at Shay, she will die." Her eyes bored into Kaireen. "The giant will come, and you will see for yourself. For now, trust that my words have healed her, some."

Chapter Twenty-one

Feoras combed his sandy hair back with his hand. The witch woman's herbs had not killed his father, but she swore on her screams he would be weakened to the point of death.

Feoras fingered the pearls on his father's sword hilt. Waited ages for this night. Years of planning, pretending, and now he would have it all.

Everything he wanted rested with this sword. Until tonight, he would conceal the sword's presence when he returned with it after meeting the Liannon spy. A sliver of the moon cast shadows across the floor.

After supper he added the witch woman's sleeping powder to the wine jug the guards drank from. With a full stomach of food, the potion would take two hours to take effect, she had said. Plenty of time for them to be stationed at their post and fast asleep. The guards' sleep would last until dawn.

Enough time to kill and avoid suspicion. The figure in the bed moaned in sleep.

Opened window shutters invited in the night air. Silk drapes around the bed billowed.

The stone floor cooled his feet. Anger built within him, boiled his blood. He adjusted his black linen cloak. How he had dreamed of this, harbored the image of his father's death for so long.

Drawing the sword from the scabbard, his victim's sword, shivers raced down his back. When Rhiannon sent word of it in her possession, his heart had leapt with joy. He would avenge the only woman who had ever touched his heart. He did not see what grew there from her bitter touch.

His mother.

Damn his father for ripping their family apart. Feoras brought the tip of the sword's blade to his lips and then kissed the metal. He could taste the blood of revenge and the wealth of the spoil to come.

Soon, he would bring her back home. His eyes misted over, imagining Rhiannon back home where she belonged.

Feoras smiled.

His brother, Bearach, would demand justice for this—his father's death. And justice would be taken from the Liannon clan and Kaireen's fair hide.

To avoid distrust, he would allow his brother a brief rule.

In the distance, an owl hooted and Feoras trembled with excitement. But all the better if Bearach died in battle with the Liannons. Have a hero's burial and the clan would look to their new laird, Feoras.

He would bring Rhiannon back to the clan, home. Together they would rule both the O'Neill and Liannon lands.

Feoras raised the sword and stalked closer to the bed. His hand trembled as he drew the curtain back from the bed post.

Clouds shifted away from the moon, lighting the room, like the heavens showed the way.

Feoras snarled and drove the sword through the body.

A gasp escaped from the victim. Feeble, wrinkled hands gripped his arms. Recognition of his killer flared in his eyes. Choking on blood, his father struggled to speak, struggled to breathe.

Feoras might end his life sooner. But the pleasure of seeing his father's pain thrilled him deeper than he imagined.

In his father's dying eyes, Feoras saw his reflection. Power surged through him as life seeped from his father.

How he longed to prolong this man's suffering. Watch his beating heart strain to continue. He left the sword in the body, proof of the Liannon clan's guilt.

Ancient Greek custom called to inhale the last breath of a dying person then you absorb their power, their prestige . . . like a blessing.

Feoras saw the light fading from the old man's eyes. So he covered his father's mouth with his. He inhaled, drawing in the last breath. Holding his father's breath, he believed the gesture empowered him. His fingers tingled. His father's blood dripped from his mouth.

This, he received as a blessing from death, of his succession in the clan. Feoras would rule, as his mother promised him.

The first step was completed. His father was dead.

Eventually, he would rule all of Ireland. First would be to break the Liannon clan under his will. Feoras yanked the black hood back and then crept from the room.

A leer froze on his face and he mused if anyone saw his expression, they would run the other way. In his hand he held a torn piece of cloth he stole from the Lochlann the day of the battle they fought for that girl. He left it wedged in the door to his father's chamber.

Stepping over the sleeping guards, he snuck back into his chambers.

Inside, he undressed. He wiped his mouth and tossed the blood stained cloak into the hearth. The fabric caught on the flames and then crinkled into ash. He removed each garment he wore and threw them one at a time into the flames until he stood naked before the hearth.

All was well. His father was dead. And he was reborn.

Chapter Twenty-two

Since Shay's stillborn son, Kaireen's parents had given her a reprieve from her punishment to rest and mourn with her sister. She was allowed three and half days before she would be sent to work at the monastery. In truth, she would have been glad to leave as planned.

No longer did Bram kiss or hold her. For hours at a time, he would disappear, and she found herself wandering the halls unable to sit still. Where did he go? Perhaps he was indeed the spy?

In such a short length of punishment, she had forgotten simple freedoms like having time to herself. She was supposed to be keeping her sister company, but disliked hearing her talk nonstop about her new husband to be and from what country he would be from since they would be on a ship most of their marriage. Kaireen wanted to strangle Elva for putting lunacy into her sister's head. After she broke her fast with her sister, she could hear no more and would take her leave for the rest of the day. Her sister didn't seem to mind and would continue her story wherever she had left off the day before the next morning.

In the courtyard, she spotted Bram teaching Megan swordplay. They used wooden swords and she could tell he sometimes let her niece win, and would encourage her when he did not.

"What has you smiling so?," he asked.

"I'm just remembering my father and how he taught me."

"With swords?"

"No. Well, a little. It was mostly with the bow. I could shoot any target." She laughed remembering. "But I could not sew straight no matter how hard I tried. I think because I was strong like the son my father always wanted, he taught me things like archery and a little with the sword. This he never did for my other two sisters. Mother was scandalized when she found out about it."

"Why? Sometimes it's best if a woman knows how to fight. In my country we have shieldmaidens who fought in battles and are heard about in our legends and sagas."

And she had no doubt they did. An image of her and Bram's daughter, if they were to marry, popped into her thoughts. She would have golden hair like her father and would wield the sword better than him and carry a bow with her everywhere she ran. Kaireen shook her head.

"Care to have a go?" He waggled his sword toward her.

"Why not?"

They spared and joked the afternoon away. Kaireen laughed so much her stomach hurt. But not once did Bram mention their wedding or attempt to kiss her. She felt as if a weight had lifted off her shoulders.

...

More and more Bram filled Kaireen's thoughts during the days and nights. She would now wake in the middle of the night and long for his arms around her as he had in her dream. Since the day of Shay's stillborn lost on the cliffs, he had not once tried to touch her. She missed his kisses more than she wanted to admit. Now there was less than a day left before she would complete her time at the monastery. Her parents were throwing another dance this evening to send her off for her last punishment before she was to marry. They still had not relented in their wishes.

Elva dressed her in an emerald gown that hung too low for her tastes. She colored when she wondered what Bram would think of the dress. After her hair was tied back, she stood. This would be the last night she would see Bram for days. Part of her was relieved, but another part buried deep inside her missed him already. She thought about bringing her dagger, but dismissed the idea. With Bram recent actions as though resigned not to touch her body or lips, she did not think it necessary to bring the blade to the evening meal.

At the great hall, Kaireen picked at her food. Bram sat at another table with Rebecca on his right. She was back at her parent's high table. They did not seem concerned that he did not eat the evening meal with them. After what seemed like the meal was never going to end, the servants moved the lower tables and the musicians set up for the dance. She waited for Bram to come to her and ask for a dance, but he did not. Instead, he danced with Rebecca and Kaireen's mother. Whatever he said to them made both women laugh, but it was when Rebecca giggled and put her hand on his shoulder that Kaireen stomped toward them.

"I think your leine is showing." She snapped at Rebecca.

Embarrassed, the woman scuttled off to tend her dress.

Alone except for the other dancers and musicians, Kaireen nodded to Bram and waited for him to take her hand and continue the dance. When he bowed slightly and left her, she gaped after him.

He went to the balcony where he had first tried to kiss her. Smoothing down her skirts, she followed him.

"I still think about that night when we were here last. Do you?" She bumped against his shoulder.

Only the sounds of a wood grouse, crickets, and the lively tune from inside answered.

"Bram?" Trepidation flooded her.

"I was going to tell you tomorrow, but it's probably best that you know it now."

He took a breath and Kaireen felt as if she stopped. A gnawing fear inside her made her want to double over, but she locked her legs.

"I have wronged you." He held up a hand at the shake of her head. "In my country we believe that an individual's freedom can overshadow the rights of kings. Even though I am no king, I have not given you your freedom to choose. Consistently you have told me that you do not wish to marry me. I've only wished to make you happy, and it is evident to me now that I cannot. I will honor your wishes and I release you from our marriage commitment."

"Will you and Rebec-?" she couldn't get the words out.

He grasped her hand turning it over to bring the palm up to his lips. His kiss there brought shivers through her body. "No. I will not marry her or anyone. Goodbye Kaireen and good journey in the morning."

Without another word, he left. Moments went by and she could not stand to be outside any longer. She flew past dancers, not stopping when her father bellowed her name. She ran. It wasn't until she was at her sister's bed room did she stop.

"Oh good, you're here." Her sister answered. "Stay with Megan for me? I haven't been able to dance tonight because her stomach's been ailing her, but I think she's over the brunt of it."

She nodded woodenly. Megan lay on her side with her mouth open as she slept.

Her thoughts shifted to self-pity. What was wrong with her? Wasn't this what she wanted? To be rid of Bram and not have to marry him? Then why did she feel so wretched?

Chapter Twenty-three

Bells pealed from the monastery's bell tower to signal the morning meal. Within this square sanctuary, candles stood in gold candelabras. The scent of beeswax mingled with the smell of soap, and earth from stone and wood. Oak benches lined the wooden walls. Kaireen would move the seating back after the floor dried.

Kaireen rubbed her back, never imagining a stone floor could be so filthy. She vowed to have her servants mop hers and Bram's keep once a day. She smiled at the notion.

But she had not seen him for three days since he told her goodbye. She spent those days and nights here, at the monastery.

The admittance to herself of her wanting his kisses angered her. After the first day of scrubbing the floors here like she thought the devil would rise out of a stain, she let her mind wander. It was a tedious task, but no thinking was needed to complete them. She should have felt relief at Bram's words; instead, she yearned for things she did not yet want to admit. She longed for his arms to hold her, his lips upon hers. She bit her lower lip. Had he forgotten her?

Her parents left strict instructions with Friar Connell. She should serve the church well and earn her repentance.

Friar Connell's eyes told her how excited he was to oversee her punishment. Now Kaireen no longer wondered why. They gave her all the duties no one else wanted.

She grasped the wooden bucket full of gritty water and then slumped outside. At least here it smelled of old paper, mud, and goats. She would never go to the dyes again.

The bells continued their clanging. Kaireen's felt ill at the thought of the simple breakfast they had here. Eggs, milk, and slices of bread donated from the serfs as part of their tithe. Since the last time she had seen Bram, her appetite had vanished. Still she forced the food down.

Working for hours before the sun rose did not help her appetite. Neither did it help her sleep. She tossed and turned every night.

Brisk wind flung her brown robes against her skin. The wool itched her. Another necessity for her punishment, and the damask gown she arrived in was locked away until her departure.

With one hand she shielded her eyes from the eastern sun, and held the robe away from her front with the other.

Strands of her auburn hair loosened from her braid and wisped across her face. Strange, she did not smell the eggs sizzling from the great hall, nor did smoke rise outside from the hearth.

She dumped the bucket. Water sloshed across the grass. Then she swung the bucket as she went back inside the nave.

Opening the wooden cupboard, she replaced the empty bucket alongside the damp mop.

Again the bells rang, as if they forgot they already called everyone to the first meal.

She held handfuls of her robe as not to trip and raced outside. Friar Connell prohibited tardiness. She did not want him to deny her penance served because of lateness.

She stumbled forward. Grumbling, she hiked her robe higher.

Monks scrambled through the courtyard with anxious looks on their faces. The bells' peal echoed in her ears. She winced at the sense of urgency of their sound vibrating through the air.

Friar Connell raced toward her, waving his thin arms. His face flushed. His brown robe bulged outward from the wind making his thin frame seem to skitter forward a step. He grasped Kaireen's elbow and dragged her forward.

"Did you not hear the bells?" He did not wait for her answer. "To the tower basement before they are upon us, in case they come this way after the battle."

Smoke billowed in the distance, from direction of her father's keep. Kaireen jerked to a stop. "Lochlanns attacked our keep?" Her bow and dagger were at her parent's keep. The monks did not allow women to have weapons or anyone who did penance to have them here.

"No, no." Friar patted her hand. He managed a weak smile which did not reach his grey eyes. He sighed as though realizing she was not placated by his answer. "'Tis another clan. Not sure who, but blood trails behind them."

Lead weight plunged to the pit of Kaireen's stomach. Warring clans proved worse than even the Lochlanns at times. This was the purpose of her marriage to Bram to help guard against future Lochlann and other Irish clan attacks. If she had agreed, she and Bram would have been married now and together they would have faced this foe.

She ran toward the stable with Friar Connell on her heels.

"You can do no good, lass," he panted, chasing after her. "This is in God's hands."

Inside, the monks had left the stables abandoned. Kaireen snatched her saddle from the stall wall.

Hauling the leather saddle onto her mare, the horse neighed as though sensing the urgency of her mistress.

The saddle situated, Kaireen tightened the girth underneath the horse's belly.

Friar Connell, red-faced, flapped his jaws, but she ignored him. His words drifted on the air of foolish girls and having faith.

She snatched a bridle and slipped it over her mare's head, adjusting the bit. Ready, she placed her foot in the stirrup and hoisted herself up. She settled into the saddle hiking her monk's robe out of the way and tightening her hands on the reins.

Friar Connell stood defiant, blocking her way. "Get off that horse, or you do penance for a month—married or not."

"Despite if this cost me a lifetime, I will not abandon my clan by cowering in the safety of your monastery." The chestnut mare pranced within the stall, anxious to get out and gallop. "Move, my good friar or I shall jump through you." She had to see Bram. Somehow she knew he was still at the keep, that he had not left yet. It consumed her to know for herself that he was unharmed. She could scarcely think of little else.

He harrumphed at her, but she kneed her horse forward.

With a yelp, Friar Connell dove sideways as Kaireen's horse jumped past where he had stood and raced from the stables.

But Kaireen did not know how she could help. Her bow and arrow were out of reach within her quarters at the keep. If the warring clan recognized her, they would hold her for ransom or as bait.

Ancient oaks and ash streamed passed her as her horse galloped forward. Kaireen clutched the reins, hoping to calm her nerves.

Suddenly her horse altered their path, and headed for a cluster of elm trees. Kaireen jerked on the reins to redirect her to the keep, but the mare continued on her new route.

"Turn around." She kneed the animal and tugged the reins. The horse took a few side steps, but kept on the path toward the trees.

At their approach, a group of crows took flight, cawing at the intrusion. Kaireen leaned back in the saddle to turn the possessed beast around.

Past the first row of elm and shrubs, her horse stopped within a clearing in the center of the trees. Kaireen slipped backward, landing on the ground, her horse whinnying at her for not holding on.

Kaireen rose and dusted her brown robe. "I would not have fallen if you had obeyed," she scolded her horse. Her skin prickled with gooseflesh and she rubbed her arms.

Distant shouts drifted from the battle carried on the wind. Kaireen shook her head and heard the rustling of leaves stuck in her auburn hair. She had no time for formalities.

"Enough." She strode to her mare.

To turn the stubborn beast around she tugged on the bridle. Her horse locked its legs, and refused to move one step forward.

"If you do not move this instant," Kaireen struggled with the reins, "I will leave you here and go afoot."

Still the animal would not budge.

A murmur behind her sent her heart slamming into her chest.

Had an enemy seen her and followed her? She dropped the reins, glaring at her horse for getting them into this mess, and looked behind her.

On a fallen log faded silver by time, Elva sat with her back straight and hands crossed in her lap. A bemused smile twitched at the corner of her handmaid's mouth.

Kaireen gasped. What was her handmaid doing outside, here in a splattering of trees?

She lifted her chin and resisted the urge to pluck the twigs and leaves from her hair. Perhaps her appearance caused her handmaid's amusement. "What are you doing here? You should be at the keep, preparing the heated oil to pour on our enemies."

Elva stood, unclasping her hands. The same instant, Kaireen's horse unlocked and began to graze.

"I am where I am meant to be for the moment," Elva answered.

Kaireen opened her mouth to speak, but her handmaid continued.

"And where do you think you are going? Not to battle." She tsked. "Captured or killed if you go in now."

Kaireen clenched her fists at her side. "Bram, a-and my family need me." His name tumbled from her lips. Was she to be a widow before she became a bride?

Elva clapped her hands together and Kaireen jumped. "You fell for the lad. It's etched across your heart, for all who can see to see." She chuckled.

Kaireen stomped toward her horse. "I have no time for your foolishness," she called back. Many people whipped their servants, but Kaireen never had; however, this situation gave ample thought now.

Approaching her mare, the animal skirted around her. She whirled around as the horse pranced to the other side of the silver log near Elva. Realizing her mouth was agape, she clamped it shut.

Elva stepped forward. "If you wish to save him," she took another step, "you must do exactly as I instruct."

Uneasiness crept across Kaireen. The wind stirred. Around them a fog crept through the elm trees. It drifted across the ground. The white mist covered the earth. The elm trees rustled and were swallowed by the fog.

Elva stood less than a foot from Kaireen. Yet she barely saw the color of her handmaid's grey livery.

Her pale skin disappeared into the fog as if her handmaid was never there. Elva stepped forward and clutched Kaireen's arm. She spoke of her plan and what her mistress must do.

Kaireen shifted, listening to the rantings of a madwoman.

Chapter Twenty-four

Feoras smirked at his brother's back. Their men tore through the Liannon clan. Revenge fueled their swords.

In front of him, Bearach slew two of Liannon's clansmen. Their blood spewed in an arc. Bearach roared as though he were a berserker. Then he bound for another man who attacked one of his sons.

Feoras frowned. Best if Bearach's sons died in battle with their father. If they managed to survive, their death would be arranged later. They were more stupid than their father.

The clanging of metal swords and shields vibrated through the air. His men breached the outer walls and filtered in through the gateway.

Left of the gateway's column tower, women lifted a steaming cauldron. As the O'Neill's passed, the women aimed the hot oil and drenched men below.

The screams of horses and men drowned out Bearach's warning bellow as he hacked through the crowd of Liannon a foot away.

Scalding oil fried the men's skin raw. In crackling heat, skin burst and the sizzling of flesh echoed with the stench of burning bodies. Fiery arrows shot from the slits in the walls igniting the oil as they passed the gate.

Feoras kicked his horse into a run. With his shield he dodged swords and arrows. Past the gate tower, he set his horse to a gallop. His destiny would protect him from the burning oils. Seconds later, he passed the gate tower and then heard the crash of two boulders drop behind him. "For the death of Laird O'Neill and the reign of the new laird!" he called to his clansmen and raised his sword high.

His men repeated his words in a shout. Following Feoras, they stormed ahead to the keep.

Laird Liannon had placed a majority of his soldiers to defend the gateway. It was not enough to defeat Feoras. He and a few men had breached it.

When Feoras captured Kaireen, he would force the Liannon clan to bow.

Besides, Feoras smiled as he sliced a peasant who raised an axe at him, the laird and his wife would die soon after Kaireen.

No peace would be made with the Liannon clan. The death of Laird O'Neill dissolved the pact. All those in authority and their families would die. The servants and peasants would be given the option of pledging fidelity of slavery to the O'Neill's and would live if they did so.

The O'Neill's would keep fighting until Feoras yanked their necks to stop. Previously, Bearach, blinded by rage, promised to deliver the guilty ones from the Liannon clan.

Feoras wished he could have witnessed the look on his brother's face when he saw their father's sword protruding from the old man's chest.

A pregnant woman screamed before he realized his horse had trampled her. He shrugged, one less Liannon bastard to feed when he became ruler of these lands.

He straightened in his saddle. Today, he would make his mother proud of him.

Today, he rescued her from her life of servitude and restored her to the laird's side as she was meant. The O'Neills were punished because of tossing her away, but the Liannons were to be crushed beneath his heel for making her a servant. They knew she was the former wife of the Laird O'Neill and yet they treated her like a slave.

Bearach would argue her return, but it was why he would die nobly in this battle.

Soon, when they were alone with his mother, Feoras' sword would drive into his brother's guts. He would take in Bearach's last breath and capture his strength.

Vultures circled the carcasses of O'Neill and Liannon clans. From inside the keep, children and women wailed as though knowing banshees joined them while death hovered near.

An arrow rang from the east wall and Feoras lifted his shield to deflect the shot. Thirty men fought next to him, cutting down anyone in their path. He tasted the copper taint of blood on his tongue as blood soaked the ground around them. The taste of it and power invigorated him.

His clansmen would tell all he breached the keep first. Those who opposed him must hold him worthy of laird after Bearach was killed.

At least, he would offer to hold the throne until Bearach's sons were older and more carefully trained. If they lasted that long.

The gates of the keep stood locked.

"Aim the grappling hooks!" Feoras shouted.

All rushed to obey. They tossed the iron hooks at the top of the gates. The men threw the lines several times until all the hooks dug into the wood frame. Then his men tied the lines to their horses' saddles.

"Heave!" Feoras circled his horse around for a better view.

The men kneed their mounts forward. The horses' nostrils flared and muscled coats sweated from the strain.

Feoras tossed his hook among the others. To rip open the gates, he forced his horse along with the others. Pieces of wood splintered, erupting from the barricade. Grappling hooks fell with hunks of wood.

Again the men threw their hooks, and they sank deeper. Feoras urged the men forward. Soon the gates would break. As if in answer to his thoughts, the gates groaned as though a sleeping giant awakened.

Feoras whipped his horse with the blunt of his sword and the animal lurched forward. He shouted for the men to push their horses farther.

The men nodded, wiping the sweat from their brows.

Then the gates burst open, sending planks of wood and hooks flinging through the air.

Feoras cut the rope holding his grappling hook and jerked his mount around.

Horseless, O'Neill men gathered the grappling hooks and then followed behind the others to the gate.

Feoras and his men poured through the fallen gate. He wondered which room housed his mother's quarters. Surely she watched his arrival from a safe window. His smile lit his dark mood until movement in front of him caught his eye.

Greeting them in the keep's courtyard waited Bram the foreigner, and forty of Liannon's men.

Clever, Feoras thought and twisted his reins around his fist. The leather creaked as he pulled the straps tight.

Or the Lochlann got lucky. Either way it would be a slaughter for them. Liannons must not know Feoras was invincible. His mother had told him of this foreigner who was called Bram.

Bram's mare whinnied. As if for reassurance he patted the horse, and Feoras longed to say the horse had more sense than its rider.

Silence lingered as the men glared at each other. Feoras grinned and Bram lifted an eyebrow.

But Bram stole the silence and rushed forward, shouted for the attack.

Feoras' face heated. How dare the foreigner jump ahead of him. "Fight!" He gritted his teeth and kicked his horse into a gallop.

Perhaps he would give this Bram's head as a trophy to his mother. Or let his clansmen rip the man apart like jackals. It would be easy enough to convince his men, Bram was the guilty one who killed their laird at the orders of Kaireen.

Men blurred in blood and sword. He shouted an unintelligible word as he braced for Bram's attack. Yells and the sound of galloping horses choked the air.

Bram's sword clashed against his shield as he countered the blow. Yet, as if unconcerned his blade had not drawn blood, Bram laughed, spinning his sword.

Furious, Feoras swiped his blade downward. He would not let this foreigner beat him. "Jarus," he called. Where was that damn man?

He knew he would not last long if he had to fight the Lochlann, so he planned to use Jarus to help shorten the odds.

His mother would be so proud of this strategy. Everyone has a purpose, she told him. And his was to be laird and leader, whatever it took.

The Lochlann would pay for his arrogance.

Chapter Twenty-five

The enemy swarmed around Bram. He gave shout and the Liannon clansmen flanked his sides.

Feoras' brow furrowed. He swept Bram's sword back with his. "Now, do it now!" he shouted.

A man behind Feoras jumped from his horse and then rushed forward. He slashed through men.

The little man crept behind him, but Bram spared little attention for the man as Feoras slashed at him nonstop. Obviously, they thought to use this Jarus as a distraction.

But Bram would not turn his back on the enemy before him. The man was one of the leaders of this attack. If he defeated him, perhaps the others would listen to reason.

But this man's eyes were narrowed as if he planned something. *Never turn your back on a cornered rat,* he thought. Fitting, for this man's pointed nose and beady eyes reminded him of rats.

Bram heard shouts through the battle of their laird murdered.

"Kill the Norseman."

"Vengeance for our Laird."

He countered a blow with his sword.

He kicked aside an O'Neill before the man slashed his sword. Then, his horse screamed and buckled beneath him.

The little man, Jarus stood behind him and his fallen horse, bloody dagger in his hand. The man had hamstrung their horses before Bram realized it.

"Get him!" Bram cursed. "He's maiming the horses."

Jarus dodged a blade and crept toward another mount.

Bram leapt off his wounded horse. Horse wails answered him and he knew the injury was permanent. He forced his blade, into the main artery in the neck, ending the animal's suffering. "Form a shield-wall," he yelled, but the others were too far away.

The enemy swung like a blind man, as though attempting to distract him while his comrade slashed into other horse's legs.

And the Irish talked of the Lochlanns as barbarians. Bram thought. Not long ago, these same clansmen rejoiced in the joint defense of the shoreline.

Now, they come after us with murder in their hearts. He knew the sword Kaireen had brought back had gone missing.

And he heard Bearach roar that the same sword had killed his father. He demanded justice. Tears streamed down Bearach's face, coating his dark whiskers.

But this man before him, Bearach's brother, his pale eyes gloated at his brother's words. Bram whirled around, his sword searching for blood.

•••

Feoras backpedaled, seeing the determination on Bram's face. His teeth bared. Blond hair framed his head and shoulders as a mane, giving the impression of a wild beast set on killing.

A head or two taller than the others, Bram was an easy mark. The muscles in his legs and arms bulged underneath his tunic and chainmail.

Feoras knew that in a struggle of strength, with no weapons he would lose to Bram. But he must not be defeated, could not be. His mother watched from somewhere.

His heart felt stabbed at the thought of her disappointment if he failed. No. He would not fail. If he must he would take all to the cliffs with him, dashing bodies against the rocks.

Feoras pushed one of his clansmen in front of him towards Bram. Stinging sweat crept into his eyes. "Kill the Lochlann!" he screamed. "He bragged to me he murdered our laird."

Frenzy pulsed in the air among the O'Neill clansmen.

Bram stopped for a moment and then shook his head.

Men poured through the gates, echoing the cry of 'kill the Lochlann'. They piled on top of him. They kicked and punched anything moving or resembled Bram's yellow tunic splattered with blood.

Chapter Twenty-six

Kaireen hung on as her chestnut-colored mare raced to the shore. She cursed. Uneasiness bubbled in her stomach.

When she thought her breath would cease from fear, she tried to turn her mare about, but to no avail.

She dreaded what awaited her upon her lands. Part of her hoped Elva was mistaken, the other knew this was her clan's last chance for peace. Perhaps her only hope to save Bram.

She passed the circle of trees, remembering her conversation with Bram about fairies . . . of his kiss here within her homestead. Her tongue tingled at the thought, and caught the saltwater in the air.

Outside her home—their home after they married—wandered giants. Elva spoke truth. Thirty Lochlanns towered around her home.

One chopped firewood, another chased chickens back into a coop. Others folded themselves across the porch. A dozen more carried a dragon ship on their shoulders.

A ship painted with blue and white swirls. On the bow a red dragon head with gold eyes stared at her.

Her horse skidded to a stop and then sidestepped at the sight of the dragon's head moving straight towards them.

So far, her handmaid's hunches proved right, if her ranting could be called hunches. She hoped the pattern continued.

Doubt snatched her breath away. What if these were raiders? They would sail away with her, leaving Bram to die. Or worse, she thought, he may believe she abandoned him.

In turn, each man looked at her and then nudged the man next to him. Contagious silence shifted around the men until all stood watching her.

The dragon ship was set against a grassy knoll.

Sweat rolled down her back. The friar robes itched her skin, but she dared not move. The rope belt across her middle became too constricting. She forced her breaths.

"Are you men," she cringed, hearing her voice squeak, she straightened her shoulders, "friends or enemies of Bram?"

They stared at her and then each other. One of the giants loomed closer. His red hair was like burning embers caught the sunlight.

Her horse skittered and he snatched the reins. "Who is you?" He spoke in broken Gaelic and Norse. "Friend or foe of Bram?"

"Wi—er, friend," she corrected. How easily the word wife wanted to tumble from her lips. Curse Elva thrice for this nonsense.

He grinned, which Kaireen could not tell if it was from happiness or cunning. Then he hauled her to him and she shrieked.

Before she drew another breath to scream, he gave her a hug and she thought her bones were bruised.

After he released her, others took his place. Each hugged her until the last one hugged her tighter than the first.

She shook her head and then pushed against him. Like trying to knock down an oak tree. "Listen. Bram needs your help."

They looked at her puzzled.

"Fight. Bram needs you to fight with him." She waved her arms, pretending to wield a sword.

The man tossed her back on her horse. She grunted as her backside ached from the landing. She repositioned herself on her horse so as not to fall. Hearing leaves crunch in the distance, she glanced ahead.

From the fog, Elva appeared on a spotted black horse. She circled round Kaireen, her lips forming a taught line. "As many as I thought." She nodded her head.

Her linen head covering was gone and her grey hair flowed down her back. She appeared to Kaireen both ancient and young.

"I did as you requested. Now what?" She clenched the reins in her fists, refusing to scratch at the monk's robe. "It would take them a day or more to run to aid on foot. And the closest river flows away from my father's lands."

Elva smiled peering into the distance, to the circle of trees on the hill above them. "Ahh, here they come now. They must have stopped for drink longer than I wanted."

Kaireen stared at her handmaid. The woman had gone mad.

Surely she did not expect the fairy folk to fly them to the keep? If this was her handmaid's plan all was lost.

Any moment the banshee's keen warning of her family's death would pierce the silence. Instead, a thundering sounded from the hilltop.

Through the mist and crescendo, horses stampeded. Kaireen gaped. Together as though they had one mind, horses raced. All wore saddles and reins. They stopped as one, a foot from Elva.

Elva sat on her spotted mare, her eyes twinkled. She waved the men to the horses. "One for each of you."

Her handmaid sounded like a horse was handpicked for each of the men; as though horses ready for battle appeared all the time.

The men scampered onto the mounts.

Elva nudged her mare and the others followed her lead, but Kaireen did not see or hear any commands from her handmaid to make the beast follow. Did the beasts read minds, then?

"Wait not there with your mouth open for flies," she said. "The sands of time spill away."

Elva raced ahead. Her livery and spotted black horse cut away the fog opening a path for the others to follow.

Chapter Twenty-seven

Rhiannon smirked at the scene. From her mistress' window, she watched the battle. Both the laird and lady waited at the far end of the keep, in the west guard tower. The last place an enemy would look for them.

But Rhiannon knew. She helped Feoras drag them by their hair then rip the fine damask clothing from them.

Previous skirmishes with the O'Neill clan had created this west tower as a better concealment for them.

She may allow her master and mistress to live, as her pets. Until she received her fill of their remorse for causing her servitude here, they would answer for their snobbery to their new lady.

The Liannon clan's scattered bodies littered the courtyard.

Never again would she tend the dyes. Never again suffer the whimsical commands of the Laird and Lady Liannon.

She would be lady of the Liannon and the O'Neill lands.

At seeing the Lochlann's horse collapse beneath him, she clapped her hands in joy. Leaning forward on the stone windowsill, she watched.

She hated not seeing her husband die . . . the void of death in his eyes. If it had not been for her son, the man might have outlived them all.

She fingered the purple velvet dress she now wore. Snatched during the laundering, as she knew her mistress would not have the chance to ask for it again.

She told the laundry women her mistress wanted the gown straightway. But she lied to Lady Liannon, telling her she caned the launder maids for ripping the fabric.

Rhiannon tailored the violet gown to her measurements. She would grace her subjects as the lady. Her hair was stretched tight in a bun. She smoothed her grey hair to ensure no strand shifted its way loose.

Soon she would meet her loyal clansmen, loyal men to her son and her. Then, they would take the west tower.

And to ensure the Liannon clan's cooperation, and avoid any future uprisings, Kaireen, the foolish girl, would be wed to her son.

As soon as she birthed a son, she would die in childbirth.

Rhiannon would rather another wife for her son, Rebecca or Constance. Both would be manageable. Neither would vie for her son's attention with her.

But Kaireen was too strong minded, unbecoming of a lady. Rhiannon would pay for herbs to get her ripe with child on their marriage night with a son.

After nine moons, she would be rid of her. An O'Neill midwife would deliver the babe into the hands of his new mother. And she would ensure Kaireen would never hold her son. Never force her taint upon the child.

Simple enough for her to die after the birthing. No one would be suspicious. Herbs would cause her to bleed out her life, unable to wake from fever. The midwife would be her witness to Kaireen's failing health.

Rhiannon would have a future laird to raise. Would mold him as she had Feoras. And he would reign after his father when the time was right. He would rule all of this land and conquer others.

He would be better than her son, whom she had not been able to raise through adulthood. Because of her meddling husband, she was forced to abandon her son, her clan.

Movement from the corner of her eye outside caught her attention. She chided herself for not watching the battle. This was her and Feoras' victory. They would sing ballads of his triumph by the fire.

She wanted this scene etched in her mind forever. Turning back to the window a gasp escaped her. She straightened, rubbing her eyes against the mirage.

Men fought, oblivious to all, except killing their foe. High in her mistress' chambers, she saw everything.

Feoras laughed as men piled onto Bram. Did her son not see the eerie fog creeping around them? From all sides of the courtyard, as though stalking them?

The courtyard was not engulfed in the mist yet. Edges of the mist rose and fell; slithering like a snake underneath a sleeper's bed. Rhiannon watched, frozen, as the fog thickened, and spread further until it concealed everything.

Chapter Twenty-eight

Kaireen slapped away a piece of her auburn hair. Willing her mare to keep in view of Elva, she snapped the reins.

A glance around her, she found that the Lochlanns matched her pace.

Yesterday, she would have never thought to race alongside their kind. Now they were her only hope to save her family—and Bram.

In the distance, the fog enclosed as a wall after the last man hurried forward.

Elva.

If they survived this battle, and Bram lived, she would have a long discussion with her handmaid. No slipping round the matter like the woman normally did.

She prayed their horses swifter. Their horses' huffs and pounding hooves resonated through the trees.

Miles stretched on and on 'til Kaireen thought they must have reached the other side of Ireland by now.

The Lochlanns galloped with her. All watched for signs of the enemy. Beside her the flame haired giant rode. She worried the gelding he rode strained with effort carrying the massive man.

At her stare, he gave her a quick smile. She smiled back then focused on the trail ahead.

She thought of Bram. He must stay alive. She tried to ignore the vision clouding her mind of his body stiff among autumn's leaves. The red leaves blended with his dried blood, gold and yellow poorly mimicking his hair. Her heart, the broken brown leaves.

She bit her lip, then prayed he was still alive. How could she have believed she might marry another? What if Bram did not want her any longer . . . she could not bear to love without him.

His kisses, his smiles, and the way the blue in his eyes swirled as though in merriment when he goaded her.

Grief gripped her heart. It squeezed until she thought she no longer breathed. Tears threatened, but she forced them back. She hunched, and the pain lessened.

Damn her for a fool. She loved Bram and nothing would change her love, not even her stubbornness. Love had found a path around her willful heart. She ached to find Bram alive, at least to tell him of her love.

And she did not care if words of love ever crossed his lips, since he had never told her of his love, so long as he lived. Hadn't he shown her in other words and his deeds of his love? She wondered why he never said the words; I love you, to her. Perhaps he dreaded her temper and thought she wouldn't believe him.

The giant pointed to broken bodies lining the path.

Liannon and O'Neill carcasses lay around them. O'Neill's? Why would they attack?

Before she was born, the two clans had lived in peace. Decades ago they fought, but the new laird had worked to end the feuding.

Together, they had defeated the Lochlanns who threatened Bram at the invasion on her lands.

Why did they fight now? Her horse skirted around one who moaned in agony. A Liannon, Marc. He was three winters older than she.

They could do nothing for him. His wound spilled his insides and it was only a matter of minutes before he died. The giant beside her ended his suffering with his sword. Kaireen turned her head away to keep her stomach and out of respect for the man.

Another mile. Bodies marked the way. Soon they would be in the mist of the battle.

But before Elva, the fog was as thick as a stone wall. Kaireen saw nothing but her group.

She strained to listen. The faint sound of men's shouts and swords crashed in echo through the fog.

Where was Bram? She wanted to leap from her horse and call his name. Search the keep for him.

They reached the gates. Planks of gouged wood hung from the stone walls. Pieces of the gate creaked under their horses' steps.

Kaireen was shocked. How did the O'Neill clan make their way this far in?

By now, they may have possession of the keep. The arrow slits in the walls were fewer here. Her father had thought it useless to have so many holes for arrows and had ordered the ones here in the courtyard sealed with rolled glass.

No doubt Bram would fight their enemy until they killed him. He would never allow them to pass unless . . . she choked back the bile rising in her throat.

Part of her wanted to find his body and wail her sorrow to the heavens. The other refused to think on such things.

Why had the fates given her love, only to take him away? A sob escaped her throat.

Elva spun her horse around. With her finger, she asked for silence.

Her handmaid smiled at her nod and then gestured them to the left, through the courtyard.

Following Elva's zigzag paths through the fog, they maneuvered closer to the keep.

Then Elva pointed to the group of Lochlanns, directing them in silence around an oak tree. They were in the courtyard now. The oak tree shaded stone benches.

Clashes of shouts and metal resonated round them, yet Kaireen saw nothing but Elva and the other Lochlanns.

"You shoot?" the Lochlann beside her asked, waving his bow before her.

"Aye." She nodded.

He gestured to another and gibbered in their foreign language. The man was thinner than the rest. He frowned at whatever his companion said, but then grasped his bow. After thrusting the bow into the giant's outstretched hand, his quiver of arrows followed.

With a smile the red giant handed her the long bow and quiver.

She thanked him and then strapped the leather pouch around her side. She knew she must appear a sight. Dirty from cleaning the monastery, twigs and fragments of leaves poking through her hair, and dressed in a friar's brown robes, the waist cinched with a rope belt.

The Lochlann unsheathed his sword.

Kaireen knew they were in the center of the battle. Yet, due to the fog, no one knew of their presence.

Perhaps they had a chance after all. The enemy would not expect reinforcements. And certainly not as though they fell from the sky among them. She tested the strength of the bow, a little too taunt for her liking, but she would make do. She must.

She whispered a prayer for Bram. Let him be safe. Let her arrows fly true.

If he died, then she would die in battle with him. She was ready now to face whatever demons possessed the O'Neills to fight.

And she was ready to face her love. Face Bram with love in her heart and her words.

Elva clapped her hands and the mist fell away.

Chapter Twenty-nine

Liannon and O'Neill clansmen stumbled. They watched the fog crawl back to whence it came.

Elva lowered her arms. "Kaireen!" she shouted pointing, to a mound of men three strides from her. "Underneath their squirms lays Bram."

Kaireen did not waste a moment contemplating if her handmaid spoke truth or not. Instead, she nocked an arrow, and then sent it sailing into an enemy's back. Grateful the tension of the bow was not beyond her strength.

All around her Lochlanns, O'Neill's, and Liannon fought.

"The Lochlanns are on our side!" At Kaireen's words, the Liannon clan did not battle with them, but accepted their help.

Another arrow flung into a man's shoulder within the pile. She wanted a sword to hack the men who concealed her beloved.

The red Lochlann jumped from his horse. He slashed through men, making his way to the pile of squirming bodies.

After he placed his sword in his scabbard, he grabbed a man in each hand, banged their heads together and then tossed them backward.

Kaireen nocked a third arrow. She scanned the field, aimed to shoot any enemy who came too close to the giant.

Five more bodies flew past her. Three more men scampered away from Bram as the giant stretched to snatch them. They did not turn back as they raced across the courtyard.

Bram laid still, his tunic covered in blood. She slid from her horse and then ran to him.

His flesh was cold to her touch and she screamed. She knelt beside him cradling his arm to her chest.

She thought of all the words she never spoke. Her love she refused to admit. He must not die without knowing the truth. Words tore from her throat through her sobs. "I love you, Bram. I-I tried to come sooner." Oh, she'd crush Elva's neck for this, for making her a widow.

She hollered when she was yanked backwards by her hair. She fought whoever seized her, her eyes never leaving Bram's body. With a curse, she was released. Then she crawled back to him letting her lips touch his.

A glint flashed in the sun and a blade of a sword waved passed her face. The sword's edge came below her chin pressing her away.

"If you wish to save your lord father and mother," Feoras' voice whispered in her ear, "you will come with me."

Cold steel brushed her chin. A shudder ran through her, making her tremble.

Feoras jerked her by her arm and pulled her back with him. With his sword under her chin, his other hand clutched a dagger. He dragged her toward the west guard tower.

When one Liannon tried to block his escape, Feoras threw the dagger at him. The mark hit true, and lodged into the man's throat.

How many would die because of her? she thought. Kaireen glanced to Bram's lifeless body. A gasp escaped from her lips.

At his side, Elva kneeled, pounding her fists upon his chest.

The blade pressed into Kaireen's neck and she felt the stinging trickle of blood. She watched in horror as Elva covered Bram's lifeless mouth with hers.

Bram was dead. Why did Elva suffer Bram with these atrocities against his body?

"Watch it, wench," Feoras said. He did not notice Elva nor care.

She felt the drying of her blood, sticky upon her neck. Kaireen wished she could die. Her chest spasmed with each breath. *Bram*, her thoughts screamed. How could she endure this torture?

Never would she love again. Love was too raw, too deep. She would help her mother and father after the battle nursing them back to health. Her hopes for marriage and happiness of her own flew away with Bram's spirit as he approached the heavenly places.

Then she would join a convent as a nun. She chuckled at the irony. At least she was dressed in a friar's cloaks, ready for servitude.

Chapter Thirty

Inside the west guard tower, Kaireen stumbled on the stairs. Feoras climbed after her with his drawn sword between them.

Torches had been snuffed along the stone walls. In the darkness, Kaireen fell. Feoras hissed a reprimand to her. So she groped along the stairs with one hand against the wall, the other held her wool robe. She thought about throwing herself down the stairs against Feoras. But she doubted he would die from the fall. And no doubt the sword point would find its way into her. They came to the door at the top of the tower. It was locked.

Feoras shoved her aside, and then banged on the door.

Kaireen knew her family huddled inside.

But she would not cry out for them. Even if he sliced her until nothing was left. Her family would be safe.

He turned and watched her. The shadows elongated his nose and chin, making her step backward. Coldness filled his expression. "Feoras has arrived," he shouted.

Kaireen opened her mouth to protest his insanity. Her family would never open the door to an outsider.

At hearing the iron bar slide open, she jumped. What were her lord father and mother doing? Had they lost their senses?

"No!" She screamed.

But the door creaked opened and then Feoras jerked her inside with him.

As Kaireen's vision adjusted to the room, she saw Rhiannon slam the door shut behind them.

Her mother, father, and Shay were tied with ropes and sat along the far wall.

Cloths were stuffed into their mouths. Two O'Neill clansmen stood guard.

Her mother's handmaid and Feoras hugged each other and then kissed each other upon the cheeks. They spoke like long-lost friends.

Kaireen ran to her family. Her father's was face was red and sweaty, as though he strained to holler. The whole side of his face was swollen and a dark shade of purple. He was bent over and holding his side. Her mother's red-gold hair was disheveled and her left eye was swollen shut and a cut on her lip had dried blood.

Shay appeared the least disturbed. She was tied and gagged like the others, but looked not as if she fought. Instead, her blond hair shone like rays of the sun. Kaireen smelled the hint of rose perfume. Did she dress so because of Elva's words, or to look her best for the battle?

Where was Shay's daughter, Megan?

Gathering her robe, she knelt in front of them. She eased the linen strips from their mouths. "What darkness is this?"

"Rhiannon." Her mother spoke first, shifting on the stone floor. "She is behind this. Behind it all-she's the traitor we've been searching for. I should have listened to your father when he did not want to take her in."

Her father spit the last piece of wet linen from his mouth. "Damn their clan to the tenth generation."

"Careful," the guard to his right waved an axe, "or our Lady Mistress may ask your head removed if you cannot keep your mouth shut. She is the now Lady of this keep and you will address her as such."

Her father sputtered, but then acquiesced.

"Lady Mistress?" Kaireen looked around the tower. "The O'Neill clan has no Lady Mistress. The laird is th . . ."

The guard snatched her by the arm and dragged her to Rhiannon.

She stood in front of her mother's handmaid, confusion in her eyes. Long ago when Kaireen had been about Megan's age, Rhiannon had come into her clan, an outsider, an O'Neill. She had grown up with the woman around and never thought to question why she was allowed to live here. But surly—

Rhiannon's stare was hard like quarry stones. Her taunt skin was pulled tight by the grey bun of her hair. She nodded to the guard, who kicked the back of Kaireen's legs, forcing her to kneel.

A gasp escaped Kaireen at the sight of her mother's velvet gown on this servant. "My mother's . . . " she said as the guard twisted her arm.

"Do not speak unless addressed from her lady mistress," he seethed.

"My son and I rule here now," Rhiannon leered. "The fight is nearly done and we triumph."

Had everyone gone daft? "You have no authority here, nor anywhere." Kaireen shook her head as it couldn't be true. Why would her parents allow a Laird's wife — ?

Rhiannon smacked Kaireen with the back of her hand. In her mouth, she tasted her own blood. She spit the blood upon Rhiannon, and again she was slapped.

"You have the manners of swine." The older woman swept her hands across the velvet fabric of her stolen dress. "Now, I am the late laird's wife. Not that I expect you to understand. Feoras is my son and rightful heir."

Kaireen twisted around to see her family's reaction, but the guard held her in place by her arm, which throbbed like hooks jabbed into her.

"Once my mother is returned to her clan," Feoras gleamed, "and rulership established, we will deal with you." His leather boots slapped across the stone floor to her. With a fist full of her auburn hair, he jerked her head back. "You and your Lochlann killed our laird with his own sword. I pity not the death our clansmen will give you."

The sword? Aye, she had been so busy she forgot. The sword was in her room, last she knew.

Feoras forced her head in a bow to his mother. Then he swaggered away. The guard dragged her forward, after Feoras and his mother.

At swordpoint, the other guard led the rest of her family from the tower.

As Kaireen descended the steps, she wanted to kick the guard beside her who would not let go of her arm.

But the sword Feoras spoke about itched beneath her skin like a rash that would soon show upon her flesh. Why did his words sting her so?

What happened with the sword? She searched her memory. When Elva braided her hair before her punishment, the sword was safe in her—

Wait. Then Rhiannon came to escort her to her parents for their judgment.

Rhiannon. She must have seen the sword and taken it.

Fear plummeted into her stomach. This was why the O'Neill's attacked. They believed she used the sword to kill their laird. Rhiannon had framed her, but only she knew the truth. Now every man, woman, and child of the O'Neill clan would want her dead.

Chapter Thirty-one

Bram groaned as cold breath filled his lungs. Ribs bruised and broken screamed with each movement.

The sun hid behind white clouds, rays reaching through. He smelled grass, blood, and lilac.

A shadow blocked his view of the sun and he flinched. Searing pain gripped his breath. He squeezed his eyes shut, waiting for the moment to pass. He could not defend himself. This enemy would run him through and not give a second glance.

The pain eased and he was able to open his eyes.

An angel appeared before him. Her white hair flowed to her waist. Her face ancient, yet youthful, gazed at him. She was dressed in a grey livery.

"Elva?" he choked.

"Shh." She brushed his hair from his brow. A medallion hung from a silver chain round her neck. Orange amber filled the stone, and silver carvings encircled the gem. Carvings like writing or symbols he had never seen before. "Everything is fine."

"Where is Kaireen?" He struggled to lift his head, but could not because a force held him.

He realized Elva's hand rested on his forehead. "Is she safe? Has the battle ended?" As if in answer, swords scraped against swords and shields, resonating through the air.

A shout drew silence from the courtyard. He lifted his head and saw Rhiannon and Feoras in the distance. Men held Kaireen, her father, mother, and sister.

Feoras waved his sword in the air. "Men, we bring vengeance for our laird." The crowd cheered. "We have released our Lady Mistress from their prison, and she is returned to us now."

Again the crowd cheered, but Bram heard grumbling among the applause.

"Our Lady Mistress!" Feoras swept into a bow as Rhiannon inched forward.

"My clansmen." She waited until the angry shouts died from both clans. "These monsters sought to destroy us. Our laird trusted me as a spy in their midst. They killed our laird, my beloved husband. Now I beseech you, take your sword and kill all of them. Leave no babe alive. We take these lands and rule them for the O'Neill's."

A deafening roar rose. Their applause died away at Feoras' waved hands for silence. "The murderous witch stands among you now." Feoras hauled Kaireen forward and Bram gritted his teeth from pain as he tried to move.

"They lie." Elva spoke.

Everyone inhaled as though waiting her permission to breathe. Bram wondered how anyone heard her when her voice had sounded like the wind to him. But the others reacted as if thunder had spoken.

Elva stood near him, although he blinked and had not seen her rise. A yew staff was in her hand.

"Servants who speak without permission will be flogged." Rhiannon cleared her throat. "Speak again and the flogging will last until you have no skin left."

"This be like your laird's?" Elva smiled and tapped a medallion hung around her neck with her free hand.

Whispers rang through the crowd.

"Stolen, no doubt from this witch by her devil laying there." Feoras pointed to Bram.

"No," Elva said, and the pressing crowd drew back. "Bearach wears his father's medallion."

Then in answer, Bearach strode forward. Blood gushed down his left arm. But he held his medallion in his right hand for everyone to see. He gazed back at Elva in wonder.

Rhiannon stuttered when Elva raised her hand in silence.

"Kings and queens must seek approval when in the presence of a Buhn-Druid to speak." She struck her yew staff on the ground and people jumped.

"You are a druid?" Kaireen frowned. "How is that possible? You are my handmaid." Surely she jested; a druid of that stature was the highest ranking of that religion. Protected and secreted even among their own kind. And a Buhn-Druid was rumored to control the hearts of kings because of their gift of prophecy and ability to turn a battle in their favor.

"And what does Druid mean in the Celtic language, but the hidden ones?"

At the handmaid's words, Rhiannon's eyes bulged. Feoras gripped his sword, but Bearach shook his head and moved to block his brother's path.

"Long ago I foresaw the injustice and calamity that would fall upon our clan." Elva stepped forward. "Although I could not change this future, I knew worse would come if I did nothing. Forty years ago, I kissed my brother goodbye and came as a servant to the Liannon clan. Not as a spy, but as a protector of both the Liannon and the O'Neill clans. They gave me work, food, and clothing."

Mumbles rose among the O'Neill and Liannon men.

"Kaireen, nor any other Liannon, or the Lochlann Bram, harmed our laird. My brother was killed by his son."

Angry shouts drowned the sounds of robins flying overhead. Kaireen stood red faced.

Elva pointed with her staff. "Feoras and his mother are the guilty ones. He has the blood of Bearach's son upon him. And even now he seeks to kill his other rival."

Everyone gasped, seeing Feoras' sword facing his brother's back. The tip pushed through the chain mail. Bearach twisted away and raised his sword to his brother's.

Bram struggled to move, to reach his sword that lay at his feet. But as he lifted his head, he saw his leg twisted at an angle. He wriggled, groping for the hilt. His muscles convulsed from the burning pain ripping through his leg. He clenched his jaw, fearing to breathe until the pain subsided. He heard someone shouting.

"Do not move!" Feoras jerked his arm toward Elva. "Witch. She blinds you to the truth. Poisons your thoughts against us."

Kaireen took a step forward, but Rhiannon grasped her arm.

"Feoras," Rhiannon clamored as though ensuring everyone heard her. "This one holds your sword by her witchcraft to kill my son, Bearach." She jerked Kaireen toward him.

As if planned, Feoras's wild eyes darted to her. His sword shook. He eased back, lowering the sword. "Aye, Mother." He stalked to Kaireen, and yanked her forward by her hair.

She cried out, raking her fingernails across his hand. But he dragged her forward to Elva and Bram.

Bram roared. She was in danger.

The throng pressed in closer. But Bram could not move. He could not help her. While he lay helpless, she may die before his eyes.

Feoras smiled down at him. The smile elongated his nose, causing his face to resemble a gargoyle's.

Elva stood at Bram's feet. She sidestepped and then brought her staff down on Feoras' head.

He stumbled back, releasing Kaireen. Needing no encouragement, she rushed to Bram's side as he laid on the ground, unable to console her.

Tears fell on his face as she kissed him. Elva kicked his sword and the hilt rested next to his side. His fingers dug in the dirt, but his fingertips brushed Kaireen's robes. Where was his blasted sword?

She sobbed her words. He could make no sense of them. "Kaireen, hand me my sword."

"No, Bram," Elva seethed. "This is not for you to do."

At her words, confusion rang through his mind. Damn her, while she played, Feoras stood, his sword in hand.

"You will die for that witch," Feoras snarled. "I will kill your apprentice first." His wild eyes watched as Kaireen paid him no heed, but stared at Bram.

Bram knew the look. It was the look of a madman with murder caressing his mind.

"I cannot move." He swallowed. "Take my sword," he said to Kaireen.

"I-I cannot." She looked to Elva.

"I am forbidden to draw blood." Elva took a step back.

Feoras hit Elva with his sword hilt across the face. She fell back, her head struck Bram's twisted leg and he cried out.

"You see?" Feoras waved his arm to the throng. "He is her familiar, I saw him dead. Now he lives."

The crowd yelled in agreement.

"I must slice off his head and maim her power." He raised his sword back with both hands. The blade came swiftly.

Bram saw Kaireen move from the corner of his eye.

His mouth screamed no, but he knew she could not hear him. She must not sacrifice her life for his. He wanted to knock her off balance and save her.

But the unseen force he touched earlier rushed him again, pressing his body to the ground. He could not lift his head. Wind whistled in his ears.

He saw Kaireen's face, her chin set in a stubborn lift. Her green eyes narrowed.

Feoras brought the sword down. Blood splattered across his face.

No, dear Odin, not my sweet Kaireen! Bram thought. She was part of his soul.

Suddenly, the force left him. The pressing on his chest eased. He lifted himself on his elbows, grunted from the soreness.

At his side Kaireen kneeled, his sword in her hand and her dagger plunged into Feoras' stomach.

Rhiannon shrieked, running toward Kaireen. Her hands held her purple skirts. Wisps of her grey hair loosened from her bun.

Instead of softening her gaunt face, the strands gave the impression of Caoranch, the mother of demons. "I will kill you!"

Kaireen pulled the sword back and Feoras slumped to the ground. She pointed the blade at Rhiannon using both hands.

"Stop. Or you meet Feoras in death."

Bram grinned, noticing she wore a friar's brown robes cinched at the waist with a piece of rope. He wondered how long her penitence would last for these sins.

Damn his broken body. He should have protected her, not the other way around.

"You cannot harm me." Rhiannon stared at Kaireen.

"All the Liannon and I imagine the O'Neill's who remember you will attest to your bullying. I believe what Elva, sister of Laird O'Neill, has spoken to be true." She kept her eyes on Rhiannon, but addressed the crowd. "I follow the will of you, our clansmen. What say you?"

"They need a leader to tell them what to do, not a simple girl," Rhiannon smirked.

"I agree, as leader," Bearach stepped forward, "with Kaireen. I see my father's eyes in Elva, speaks the truth. Enough blood has been shed today. We all paid dearly, I—my son." His voice cracked, but he continued. "What shall be done with this traitor?"

Shouts rang through the crowd. "Burn her. Kill her. Throw her in the pit."

"To kill her will lessen her deeds." Bearach nodded. "Tie her. We take her back home."

Angry murmurs rose from the O'Neill clan. Bearach folded his arms. "I am laird now. We throw her in the pit for her memory to keep her company. I want her to suffer every day until she dies for what she has done." He shook his head as she cursed, passing him. "Perhaps God will give her mercy, for I cannot."

Chapter Thirty-two

Kaireen trembled with memories from the battle. It had taken all of her strength to lift Bram's sword. She had hoped to deflect the blow.

Thoughts of Feoras harming Bram made the sword feel light in her hands. Somehow she knew she must keep the sword up, blocking his. Then she saw her dagger glint in the sun beside Bram. Not thinking, she let one hand off the sword, snatched her dagger and thrust it into his stomach. Relieved, and the sword heavy once more, she dropped it. Feoras stood in shock for a moment, his sword arm still raised as he gazed down at the dagger sticking out of him.

After the O'Neill's had taken Rhiannon, she bent over Bram. He was alive. And she cared not how.

He held her to his chest and she heard his heartbeat. Such a wondrous sound, and she wished to lay there, listening to the rhythm forever.

Tears flooded through her, soaking through his chain mail to his saffron tunic.

"Weep not." His hand stroked her back. "Our wedding is tomorrow."

Laughter blurted with her sobs. "No, I will not marry you still."

His frown tore into her laughter and she ceased. "I am sorry you feel that way, I will leave at dawn."

"No." The corners of her mouth twitched into a smile. "We will not marry until you are healed. You promised me a glorious wedding night. And I will not have my husband lazy, and slumbering all the time from his wounds."

"Truly?" he asked and her heart soared. "You will be my wife?" She heard the hope in his voice.

She looked into his blue eyes. Clear like the autumn sky above them. His face darkened in the sun and splattered with blood.

"Aye," she answered. "I love you forever and even that will not be long enough."

His hug knocked the air from her, but she wrapped her arms carefully around his chest, and then planted kisses on his face and lips.

"Wait." He held her hands. "I have, as your faith says, a confession."

Fear tried to choke her, but she swallowed it back down. Whatever he said, it would not change her love for him, not after all they had been through.

"I made your mother a promise." He touched her lips when she opened her mouth to protest. "Let me finish. I came to the keep weeks before you saw me. I was to be arranged in marriage to Rebecca, daughter of one of your father's noblemen for my alliance. I had tasted a glimmer of love before and prayed to the gods to find it again. So I dressed as a peasant and observed her and others. However, it was you that crept under my skin. I saw not only your feisty temper, but your compassion. I knew there was no other for me. I bargained with your father for you, and had to promise more men to come with me to protect your family and lands." He caressed her cheek. "And I would have paid anything."

She leaned into his hand. "But what of my mother? What promise do you speak of?"

He ran a hand through his golden hair. "After our agreement, I told your mother I loved you. She made me vow not to tell you unless you spoke the words first. It tore me up every time I saw you. It would have been easier to have promised to bring back a tooth from Jörmungandr, the Midgard Serpent instead."

"I would not have believed you if you told me sooner. My mother was right." She kissed him until she heard a shuffling behind her.

"Good to see you again." The red giant shifted his feet. "Found this one in the stables underneath the hay."

Bram translated what the giant said so Kaireen would understand his words as well.

Megan sucked her thumb, her other hand around his neck as she stared at him.

"How did you get here so soon?" Bram squinted at him. "You must have arrived yestereve at the holding?"

His cheeks colored. "We arrived this morn' ready to work until your lass came calling."

"They helped sway the battle."

"Aye," the giant said. "Get well, brother. Your men will not be happy with cleaning for long." He winked.

"Brother?" Kaireen glanced back at Bram.

"Younger brother," Bram grunted. "And late as always for the surprise."

"Surprise?" She frowned. What mysteries did Bram hold?

His finger stroked her cheek and she longed to lean into his gesture. He loved her. And she, God help her, loved him.

"I arranged for them to sail along the coast and ready our keep for the wedding night. Lochlanns," he said the name with a peculiar lilt as though tasting the word and finding it foul, "would be too noticeable racing across the countryside. So I asked them to stay at the holding until the wedding."

"What will you pay me to keep our mouths shut from our brothers?" The giant loomed above them.

"How many brothers do you have?"

Bram smiled tapping his chin with a finger. "Well, our oldest brother lives in Norway, he inherited all the land from our father. Erick still raids . . ."

"How many?" She poked his shoulder.

He chuckled, pulling her into his embrace. "I hope us to have as many sons."

She struggled against him. Until he answered her, she would not cease. Did the man think her daft to forget the question while he held her?

Well, she was in love, but she was not daft yet.

"Nine."

She gasped and he kissed her. Nine sons? She doubted she would live long enough to birth so many children.

Especially if they grew as large as Bram's brother.

As if hearing her thoughts, the giant laughed and sauntered away. Megan giggled with him.

Chapter Thirty-three

Winter fell upon the east coast of Ireland. Four months Kaireen waited for Bram to mend so they would both be able to dance at their wedding, and more. When Kaireen admitted her love, she did not think it would increase, yet her love blossomed more each day. It was as if once the small seed took root, it grew like a forest of ancient yew trees.

After the battle, Elva set his broken bones with oak planks and ropes. Kaireen helped hold the boards in place.

Her handmaid had him bite on leather straps. She yanked his leg back, pulling the bones straight, she said.

Sweat beaded across Bram's brow and his glare bore into Elva, but she minded not. Guards held his arms. Afterwards, when they took the leather from his mouth, his teeth clenched.

"I would like to show you the blood eagle sometime."

Elva tsked. "Do you want to hobble for the rest of life, or suffer a little pain now?"

"A little pain?" He cringed. "I hate to see what you deem more."

Kaireen lay on her bed remembering. Bram's wounds and bones had taken months to heal. In Elva's care, he healed quicker than she expected. Last week Elva took the splints off, and Bram walked with the aid of his oak staff.

Snow covered the land. Winter trees were stripped bare. Kaireen snuggled deeper under the covers. Closed her eyes, and thought of Bram's kiss goodnight and his sweet promises of their wedding night.

Bram. She bolted upright.

Today was the day-her wedding day! She jumped out of bed, gasping when her feet met the cold stone floor. She hobbled sideways as she put on her slippers.

Fire burned in the hearth, bringing forth the aroma of cinnamon. She crept to the fire, gazing at the flames.

"For your wedding day," Elva said. "The cinnamon is for prosperity, protection and passion. I thought it would go well with your earlier wedding gift of the bath. Come now. Your groom has waited too long for you."

She nodded, following Elva to the bathing chambers. Her handmaid carried a basket filled with ribbons, combs, hazel twigs, and soap. In her other hand, a new linen shift and her wedding dress. The crimson gown with the square neckline would make her skin appear smooth as cream.

...

She sank into the steamy water. Months ago she hated thinking that she would wed. Now, she had waited so long it could not happen fast enough. Her heart felt as if a dozen horses were running wild and faster with each passing moment.

After bathing and cleaning her teeth, she allowed Elva to dry, and then dress her.

The damask gown fit her curves and she loved the folds that swept to the floor.

Elva wove red ribbons lined with pearls into her hair.

Then Kaireen dabbed her neck and wrists with rose oil. She donned her pile-weave cloak.

Elva beamed with pride.

"No flowers blooming for you, for it be a harsh winter. But herbs will do fine as well." She handed Kaireen a basket of cinnamon sticks and cloves.

Kaireen thanked her, and followed her handmaid through the corridors.

In the hallway, she smelled the roasting boar mingled with onions, sage, and rosemary. She licked her lips. In her rush she had skipped her breakfast to get ready. But food would have to wait until after the ceremony.

In the courtyard, the guests gathered. Each brought a hand cake. Now each cake was piled on a blanket on the ground, creating an awkward tower.

Snow and ice hung from the trees and the cloaked guests shivered. Friar Connell nodded as they approached.

Bram was dressed in sapphire tunic stitched with gold threads.

Her breath caught in her throat. He held a hand out for her and she took it. No longer was she scared of loving this man, this Viking. Originally she had thought it was because of his heritage that she was so adamant to not marry him, but only now could she admit it was also that she feared his love would consume her. Now she could not accept a future without him.

She noticed he wore a silver necklace, the emblem shaped as Thor's hammer and cross. Her mother's eyes blinked back tears.

Kaireen shifted her feet and then looked to the Friar who nodded his approval for them to speak their vows.

Do not let me forget my words, she prayed. "Bram, I pledge my life and love to only you. I promise to always love and cherish only you. Birth you strong sons, and stronger daughters." Women in the crowd chuckled. "Honor and respect do I also give you and demand the same from you to me. I will go where you go with the grace of God."

Bram cleared his throat, his skin faded pale. "I promise you to love and cherish only you always. Raise our children with you. And not to lift my hand toward you in anger, but to protect you with my life." Then he drew her in close, brushing his lips across hers. He whispered against her mouth of wanting to fulfill all his passionate promises to her.

"By the power of God, I hereby bless this union." Friar Connell sprinkled holy water from an implement made of gold.

With the crowds' cheers, Bram and Kaireen rushed to the stack of cakes. They circled their arms around the stack, grasping their fingers, careful not to touch the cakes.

Stretching forward, she leaned on her tiptoes. They kissed over the cakes for prosperity. The throng shouted when one of the cakes wavered, but did not fall. Everyone rushed forward, congratulating the couple. Then they followed the bride and groom into the great hall. She was glad to be inside by the warmth of the hearths.

At the high table, Kaireen's father and mother sat to her right, Bram on her left.

Four servants brought silver trays with roasted boar covered in onions. Trays followed of cooked goose coated with pepper, bail, and rosemary. Gilded and slivered calves heads with roasted peacock came next with its feathers hung over the tray.

Then platters of cheeses, tarts and custards arrived. Each guest's goblet was filled with honey mead or the mulled wine the Lochlanns called spicey.

Sallat from boiled carrots, lettuce, nuts, vinegar, and oil stuffed in a wooden trencher was offered as well.

Bram's men joined in with the Liannon's laughter at the lower tables.

Kaireen ate until she thought she would burst her gown. Then the servants cleared the hall. She swirled to the round dance as long as the musicians played.

Hours flew by. Rebecca danced with one of the Lochlanns and Kaireen hoped she would find love.

Bram's brother, the giant, held Shay with his eyes and arms. He strained not to cringe at her as thrice she stepped on his foot.

Perhaps love would come to Shay again.

Already, she glowed with Bram's brother. What wonder that so much life, love and death could come through the Lochlanns. Kaireen had learned to trust her handmaid's words. How confoundedly stubborn she had been. Kaireen hoped her children might not inherit too much of her stubborn heart while Bram hoped they did fire and all.

Beside her, Bram nuzzled her ear, causing her to forget the dancing couple. He whispered her to follow him and she did.

They maneuvered through the crowd. In the corridor, he clutched her hand. He drew her with him as they ran through the hallway.

Outside her room, he winked. "Not so loud." He pushed open the door. "I think you did not want your wedding gown torn off by the crowd."

She blushed to her toes. Custom said the clothing of the bride was lucky. She remembered the horror of her eldest sister's wedding.

The guests had followed the bride and groom to their bedchambers. But they tossed and locked her groom out. Then everyone pressed around tearing away pieces of her gown. By the end, she had been left shivering and naked.

Kaireen felt a lump in her throat. The bedroom door clicked closed. No one save her maidservants had seen her without clothes.

Already, Bram stood before her, his clothes in a pile on the stone floor. His muscles were chiseled and despite his scars, she found no flaw.

Golden hair flowed to his shoulders. His full lips formed a smile as he gazed at her.

From his boldness, she glanced lower and saw a rod between his legs. She jerked her head away, her face burning.

"Well, wife?"

Her mouth went dry. "No." Last night her mother and Elva explained the marriage bed, but she imagined his implement a dagger, not this broad sword. He would surely kill her.

She hiked up her skirts and bounded to the door. But he chuckled, hauling her back by the waist.

"I promise I will not do anything unless you ask." He carried her across the room.

She squirmed in his arms. His manhood pressed against the back of her thigh. He dumped her in the bed and then held her with his arm as he dove in after her.

He kissed her neck. Then he nibbled at her ear lobe until she offered her lips.

His lips touched hers and she opened her mouth. She eased her tongue out, ran the tip along his lip. He groaned and opened for her, their tongues blending together.

Heat coursed her between her legs. He stroked her hair, her arms.

She mumbled she was hot and so he removed her wedding gown. Embarrassed, she folded her arms across her chest. Only her leine covered her.

Bram kissed her again, making her forget her worries. His hand stroked her breast, teasing the nipple through the fabric. Pleasure flooded through her. His other hand lowered to her stomach and then at the junction of her legs. She gasped as moisture pooled there.

His fingers caressed her where no one else ever touched her and she clenched the bed sheets in her fists. He continued this torture despite her whimpering until her legs grew numb. "Take off your leine if you want more," he whispered.

She jerked the leine, tearing the fabric. He leaned back, his fingers ceased their movement.

Had she done something wrong? She shivered with his body away from hers. She opened one eye watching him.

He stared at her, his breathing heavy. He saw her stare and smiled. "I wanted to see you."

She tugged on the sheets.

"No. The sun will set within the hour. Let me see you in the light afore candles are lit. For we will not sleep tonight."

He kissed her lips then traced a path down her neck. Wanting more, but not sure what, she raked her hands across his back. He kissed each breast in turn until the pink nipples perked.

His kisses lingered between her legs and she thought she would burst. Then he kissed her stomach, her breast, her neck, then her lips again.

This was madness. Her body pulsed with her want of him. What did he wait for?

"Now, please now."

He used his hand and moved his member to the junction of her thighs. Her breath forced as he sheathed himself into her flesh. She cried out against his mouth.

"Shh. It hurts this first time, that's all. But I promise I will bring us both pleasure."

She wanted to punch him. Push his invasion away. If this is what the marriage bed entailed, she wanted nothing more to do with it. She opened her mouth to tell him so, when she saw his face.

Sweat beaded across his forehead the same as when Elva set his leg as she called it. His brow furrowed in concentration and his azure eyes darkened as he gazed at her with love, pain, and wonder. Somehow, this union caused him pain too?

"I love you." The words flowed from her mouth.

"Kaireen," he kissed the tip of her nose, "I love you too. As I also promised in our vows."

Truly he loved her. Aye, she recognized the emotions in his eyes. He shifted, and pleasure mingled with pain raced through her. Where they merged, she throbbed.

Slowly, he eased from inside her, then back inside. She bit her lip, worried about the pain. But then her body rose to meet him. She kissed him, holding his golden hair in her fists.

Despite her protest, he kept the pace slow. The man wanted to drive her mad. Her muscles seized then released with her climax.

They lay together, each panting from their lovemaking.

"I love you, my stubborn bride, my sweet wife." He took her in his arms.

She kissed his chin. "And I love you." She paused. "Bram?" The room was dark and she could not see his face. "May we do it again?"

"Aye." His laughter boomed through the room. "Many times tonight and the next day, and the next. And I have Elva's promise our bathing on the morrow will be ready here with herbs to remove your tenderness."

She crept from bed and then used her flint stone to light the candles. A dozen candles splayed across the shelves along her walls. She smiled, imagining their children to come.

They would have at least three. Two girls, and a son. Aye, a son whom she would name Lochlann for his father's heritage. His ancestors would be McLochlann, son of Lochlann for generations. A sign that the word that she once thought appalling had now become her love and father of her children.

Embers burned in the hearth but she noticed kindling stuffed among the iron frame piled into ash. Logs were staked beside the hearth. She threw three logs onto the fire.

She shivered and crawled back into his waiting arms.

"Will we talk before slumber?" she asked. How long did he need to recover from their duty? She had overheard tales from the other servants . . . a man took hours to recover.

His fingertips brushed her lips, and then he followed with a kiss. "I want to see you by candlelight now." His fingers stroked her neck, and then his lips traced their path. "And in the dark, and come the dawn at our keep, and come—"

"Enough talking." Her fingers pressed against his mouth.

He smiled against her fingers and did her bidding.

More From This Author

(From **The Garnet Dagger** by Andrea R. Cooper)

I've known death. For over half a millennia, I escorted many to death at the end of my sword. In the eyes of the dying, I watched it shroud them. Foolishly, I thought many more eras would pass before death came for me. It came so swiftly that I could not run; I could not escape.

At a village, dressed in human clothes, I took in everything. By observing for eons, I understood and spoke their language. The world of mankind fascinated me. Their hobbled homes burrowed into the ground. Rocks crunched on top one another with thatched roofs woven from straw. Never had I seen a home or inn that was higher than three levels, as if they were afraid of the sky.

I delayed my return to my people as I watched human jugglers bounce torches and knifes. It was autumn equinox and the festivities would continue well into the night. Children laughed as they chased each other. A trail of leaves from their costumes twirled after them. It was dark when I reached the forest. Since I was already late, I hiked uphill to a shortcut rather than take the long path back home. I didn't need to alert any of my kind near the barrier at this hour. Liana would wonder why I was late. Tonight was the two month anniversary of our hand twining ceremony. One more month as was custom, and then we'd be wed.

A gasp rustled through the trees. The roots shot a warning through to me with stifled caution. Adjusting my pack, I continued on instead of changing back into my Elvin clothes. After I passed the border which kept humans from entering our land, then I'd change.

In the distance, I heard a groan. Curious, I spun in the direction of the sound. The autumn wind breezed through my worn human clothes, chilling me. But someone needed help. I turned in the direction of the sounds.

Whatever made the noise should be a few yards ahead. I hiked slower than my normal speed, so as not to startle whatever human called out. My leather boots crunched upon dried, diseased leaves and bark. Horrified, I glanced up.

Branches twisted around each other to suffocating. Lifeless limbs cracked in the wind. Flesh of the trees sloughed off in layers, exposing its bones. Gashes hollowed out chunks of warmth. Fragments of leaves clung to finger tips, marking sepulchers of the dying trees.

Trees mourned with wails like splitting wood, and I brought my hands over my ears. I must flee before I became infected, they told me.

Flee before the stain of this defilement creeps into you, they warned. Trees spoke to my kind, always had. Yet these trees were in such agony of death that I could not breathe. Felt as though my lungs had folded in on themselves, like a moth unable to break loose from its cocoon.

Nothing I could do for them, and if I lingered too long, whatever disease gnawed upon them may choke me. Where would I go if I carried something so foul as to devour trees from the inside out? I'd never return to Tamlon if I brought this infection with me.

I drew away, but a movement at the base of a decaying tree to my right caught me. My night vision picked up the sight of a human. His sallow face seemed to glow in the moonlight. Poking out from rags lay his arms and legs, which resembled skin stretched over sticks.

So cadaverous was his face, I'd have thought him dead if he hadn't moved.

"Please," he said and his voice sounded like cicada's vibrations, "help me."

"What ails you in this troubled place?" I wondered if my voice, foreign to my ears in speaking the human's language, revealed my nature.

"I am lost." His dark eyes crinkled around the corners. "Without strength to rise. If you would but assist me up, I'll be on my way."

I'd never touched a human on purpose before. Was it that that gave me pause, or dread that stilled my heart? My feet itched to flee. As soon as I helped him, then I'd leave. I gritted my teeth and reached a hand down.

His gnarled fingers snapped on my arm, making me wince. Jerking me forward, his face contorted. Surprised by his strength, I fell beside him. Blackness curled around me.

Teeth, fangs, broke through the skin on my neck. Then I knew him for what he was, a vampyre. I struggled in protest. My words trapped in my mind. This shouldn't happen. I was not human. But I felt my essence slip from me with each sucking sound he made.

I tried in vain to push him off me. I was paralyzed. My joints and muscles locked in place. I couldn't move. *Release. Get away.* I screamed again and again in my mind, but my body refused to obey. If I could reach my sword then I'd behead the monster. But my hands, even my fingers, refused to move.

Felt as though my bones were replaced with steel rods, which now in place, were tempered closed. Embracing death. Wind roared in my ears, bringing the laments of the trees around me, piercing into my soul. Here, I was to die.

• • •

He twitched.

And I felt a tugging at my wound. But apparently neither of us could disentangle. He was locked with me, and I with him.

Pain churned behind my eyes like scorching fire. It seeped through my skull and down my spine. His essence mingled with mine and filled me.

And I knew him.

I knew his thoughts, his name, and his victims through the centuries. Inside my head he was yelling. "Not human. Not human. What are you? Draining me, my power." His words shattered through my mind.

I didn't know what was happening. The ground beneath me sighed. Bugs crawled along the leaves, their mouths crunching through the bark. In sleep birds ruffled their feathers.

Stench of blood and death lingered. A feeling of falling coursed through me. Everywhere my skin tingled like pine needles pricked me. I sensed each groove of my knuckles.

Strength returned to me, and yet something more. A thickness settled over the beating of my heart. Just beneath my skin, an itch, a tingling.

My muscles and bones relinquished their rigidness. I shoved him away and he gasped.

"What have you done?" Black blood ran from his eyes.

"Nothing." I saw his life force shimmering like the dew in morning. Fragile and waiting for the day to melt it away.

His eyes rolled back into his head, and he was dead.

But I was alive, no vampyre. I shrugged it off that my kind must have immunity to his. Doubt tickled behind the veil of my conscious mind. Fleeting stories of prophecy and a dark monster read to me as a child.

My fingers brushed across the wound from my attack. Before I stumbled upon any other visitors, I decided to change my clothes. These human clothes had nearly killed me.

I removed my old human clothes and left them beside the rotting body. Thrust my legs into my trousers. Then I yanked my silk tunic over my head.

Images of wolves swam through my mind. They'd be upon me in two hundred paces. Why I felt they come for me, I could not explain. Never before could I sense animals so far away, or their intent. I stomped on my boots and slipped on my cloak. Leaving the discarded clothes behind, I ran.

Heard howls echo behind me. I dared not stop, but flew over the rocks to my home. I'd search the scrolls. Warning steeled my breath when I thought of approaching my parents with what happened this night. No, I must find out for myself before I spoke about this to another.

In the mood for more Crimson Romance?
Check out *The Glass Orchid* by Emma Barron at
CrimsonRomance.com.

About the Author

Andrea R. Cooper was born in Houston, Texas, and dreamed of being a writer since getting her first praise in grade school on her story about a piece of chalk. She has an Associate of The Arts Degree and has worked as a freelance writer. She lives outside of Houston with her best friend who is her husband, their three children, and lots of books.

Made in the USA
Lexington, KY
21 February 2014